Unconventional
Beginnings

J.D. KNIBBS

 FriesenPress

Suite 300 - 990 Fort St
Victoria, BC, V8V 3K2
Canada

www.friesenpress.com

ISBN
978-1-5255-5814-6 (Hardcover)
978-1-5255-5815-3 (Paperback)
978-1-5255-5816-0 (eBook)

1. *Fiction, Biographical*

Distributed to the trade by The Ingram Book Company

Unconventional
Beginnings

Chapter 1

Garth Gibbins bounced around on the air ride seat of the four-wheel drive John Deere tractor he operated over the rough ground. His dark brown hair would flick down and cover his brown eyes whenever he hit a large bump and he would have to flick it to the side. He had a slim build with a baby face that showed the faintest signs of freckles.

The field was covered with the short stalks of the wheat that had been harvested the previous fall and the ground was hard and crusty, as up until four weeks ago, it had been covered with two feet of snow. The tractor was pulling an air seeder that was planting canola seeds that would be this year's crop.

Garth enjoyed the time of solitude in the cab of the tractor: it was a nice change from the last couple of weeks he had spent cramming for his final Engineering exams at the University of Saskatchewan. Swaying in the cab with the warm sunshine coming through the windshield of the tractor was soothing, almost hypnotic, and Garth found himself fighting to stay awake.

Garth was destined to be a fourth-generation farmer on this land in Southern Saskatchewan, near the small town of Marley, that his great grandfather William had homesteaded in the early 1900's. The 160 acres had been registered by William for the $10 fee from the Dominion Government in 1905. To gain title to the land all one had to do was reside there for three years, cultivate more than thirty acres and erect a house that was worth at least $300.

The solitary made Garth's mind wander and he found himself thinking about how this piece of land had come to be owned by the Gibbins' family. The quarter section he was working on, his Grandfather called the Kilback quarter. It had been homesteaded by the Kilback family, but in the 1930's the family had been hit hard by the drought and was forced to sell out. As the old saying goes "one man's loss is another man's gain" and over the years the Gibbins' were able to acquire some of these offsetting lands as they came available and the farm had grown to its current size of just under 2,000 acres of cultivatable dryland.

Garth's father Jack and Jack's brother Dean now oversaw the operations of the farm. Garth helped out on the farm whenever he could; however, between his post secondary education and summer engineering jobs this was becoming less and less. So, when he did get the opportunity to drive the tractor for such an important job as spring seeding, he relished the chance.

As he watched the furrows of soil pass under the wheels, he noticed the dust trail coming down the grid road towards him. He had seen the dust billowing up long before he saw the pick-up truck that he knew was the cause of the dust. The truck was his Dad's blue Ford. Garth looked down at his watch, he still had over half of the field to finish before supper time, so he wondered what his dad could want. For his dad to come out to the field and interrupt his progress meant it had to be something important.

He saw the truck slow down from the road and turn into the field. Garth slowed the tractor and stopped, waiting for the truck to drive out. The truck pulled up to the tractor and Garth's dad Jack stepped out. Jack Gibbins was about six feet tall, slim and although he was not yet forty years old his jet-black hair was already showing streaks of grey.

Garth opened the door of the cab of the tractor and felt the dry heat from this abnormally hot sunny day of late April combined with the heat of the diesel engine from the tractor. It was an overwhelming sensation compared to the air-conditioned cab, so he quickly exited the cab and scaled down the ladder to meet his father.

"Hey Dad, what's wrong?" Garth asked. Jack said, "nothing is wrong. There was a phone call at the house for you. Some lady from an oil company in Calgary wants you to call her back today. I assume they probably want to interview you for a job." Garth could detect the excitement in Jack's voice as he spoke and he even thought he could see a little wetness at the base of Jack's eyes.

"I will finish up here for you," Jack said, "so you take the truck back and give this lady a call to see what she wants. I will finish this up and bring the equipment home. I took out some deer sausage for supper, so after you make your phone call you can start supper and I will eat when I get home."

Garth climbed into his dad's truck and pulled out of the field onto the gravel road. He reached down to turn the radio on as it was his dad's habit of shutting it off before he exited any vehicle. The radio came on at full blast and Garth flinched. "Someday" by Steve Earle was on, he was Jack's favorite artist. Garth chuckled of the coincidence of that song to his own situation, as the song describes a small-town boy's dream to leave the town and find his own success in the outside world.

Jack had been a great student in his own right and had ambitions of going on to get an engineering degree. When he was in grade twelve, his girlfriend Christine had become pregnant and at the insistence of both sets of parents, Jack had decided to do the "right thing" and get married and settle into a life on the farm.

Jack had married Christine, and Garth was born a couple of months later. Jack had planned to work for a few years to build up enough money to support his family and himself through university but as the years went by, so too did the opportunity. When Garth was ten, his mom and dad had separated and his mother had moved to Regina. Jack and Christine had decided it best to keep Garth in school in Marley. This was fine for Garth as he hated the city and loved the freedom of the farm. Initially, Christine and Jack had shared custody of Garth but as the years went by and Christine had children with her new husband, Garth spent less and less time with his mother to where he only saw or spoke to her a few times a year.

Garth felt that all of these things that had happened to Jack had made him push Garth to do everything Jack himself had never been able to do. Garth loved farming and thought it was a great life, but Jack had recommended Garth take engineering instead. To Garth an engineer was someone who drove a train, but at his dad's insistence he had taken the engineering classes.

As he drove, Garth wondered which company this could be that wanted to talk to him. He had been interviewed for a few jobs by various companies at the university. All of the companies were in Calgary, Alberta. Calgary was the headquarters for the majority of the oil companies who drilled and produced the wells in most of Canada.

Garth pulled the pickup into the farmyard. The farmyard that Garth and Jack lived was about 3 acres in size it contained a small bungalow house with detached garage, two storage sheds for the farming equipment and multiple grain bins. The Gibbins' were grain farmers only and did not raise livestock, so there wasn't any barn or corrals on the property. Jack had said having animals, even a dog, meant you were always tied down to the farm and made it difficult to go on holidays, as someone had to ensure they were fed and watered continuously. Garth found it interesting that, even though they had no livestock, he still could not remember going on a holiday anywhere with his dad for more than a couple of days.

Garth stepped through the doorway, closed the door and slipped out of his workboots. He then stepped into the kitchen and walked over to where the phone hung on the wall. Beside the phone was the name Victoria and a phone number with an Alberta area code.

Garth stood in front of the phone and took a moment to collect his thoughts. He felt a plethora of emotions come over him. He was excited about the opportunity, but he was also regretting the fact that the time may finally have come where he would have to leave the farm and the life he knew. Garth took a deep breath and picked up the handset, then he began dialing the number.

On the third ring a soft and pleasant voice answered, "Hello, Victoria Cooey speaking, how may I help you?" Garth envisioned she was a young attractive lady. "This is Garth Gibbins calling, there was a message left for me to give you a call," replied Garth. "Yes, Garth," she said, "thank you for calling back, I am calling on behalf of Maldere Energy in Calgary with regards to your application for a Reservoir Engineering position we had posted. We were very impressed with your résumé and would like to have you come in for an interview."

Garth's voice quivered slightly: "Sounds great when would you like me to come in?" She said, "I know you are in Saskatchewan so we would like to fly you to Calgary next Tuesday and then have you come to our offices for an interview at 9 am on Wednesday. We will make all of the arrangements. I am going to send everything to you once we hang up. Do you have any questions for me?" "No, not at the moment," replied Garth. "Great, I look forward to meeting you on Wednesday. Thank you, Garth and have a great day!" she replied. "Thank you and you as well," said Garth.

Garth hung up the phone, and a great nervousness came over him. Garth had never even flown on a plane before so the thought of all this happening at once felt overwhelming.

He sprinted downstairs to the makeshift office in the basement. He turned on the light in the office and turned the fax machine on. No sooner had the fax machine finished its warm up routine, when the fax machine began to ring. The fax machine picked up automatically and Garth started reading the papers as they came through.

All of the details were there, timing of the flights, one night at the Palliser hotel and the location of the meeting for the interview. Garth collected all of the papers and went back upstairs. He knew his dad would be very excited to see them.

Garth placed the papers on the kitchen table and turned on the stove. He pulled a skillet out and picked up the package of deer sausage and placed it into the pan. He pealed the potatoes and filled a pot of water to boil them in. Garth chuckled, this is the meal of a farmer for sure, meat and potatoes at every meal.

Once he had everything cooking, he looked out the window and saw his Uncle Dean pull up. Although Dean and Jack were brothers, they had very differing appearances. Dean had dirty blonde hair, complete with a bushy moustache and a muscular build compared to Jack's black hair, clean shaven face and slim build. But the differences did not stop at appearances as Dean had an easy going personality and was always joking around. When his Uncle Dean was around, Garth couldn't help but smile.

Dean had been a talented hockey player growing up and many people in Marley had felt he was capable of making the WHL or even the NHL. Unfortunately, tragedy had struck for Dean before he turned 16 when a wing from a bi-fold cultivator had come crashing down on his leg. His leg had broken high up on his femur and required a lengthy recovery. By the time his leg had healed enough for him to return to hockey he was not the player he once was. Dean; however, did not let this ruin his attitude and still maintained a positive outlook on everything. Dean was still involved in hockey but now it was in coaching the midget team in Marley and helping out as the Marley rink custodian. To those townsfolk that remembered how well he could play before his injury he was still considered a bit of a celebrity in town.

Dean came up the steps and poked his head through the door. "Jimmy!" he yelled. Jimmy was a nickname that Dean had given Garth when he was a toddler. Dean said the name came from when Garth was a toddler. If he was given a toy he would take it apart and "jimmy" with it to figure out how it worked. When Dean found out Garth was accepted to Engineering, he told Garth: "I knew then that you were damned to become an engineer, you poor bastard."

"Jimmy," said Dean, "I had stopped out at the tractor to see if you wanted to go into town tonight and I was surprised to see your Dad. He said he sent you home to make a phone call or something?" "Yeah, I had to come home to phone some lady in Calgary about a job interview," said Garth. "They are sending me to Calgary next week to meet with them." "They are flying you to Calgary?" said Dean. "Yes, I leave on Tuesday and meet with them on Wednesday," said Garth. "Then we should definitely head into town tonight and celebrate," said Dean.

"That sounds great. How about 9 o'clock?" asked Garth. "Right on, I will come back later and pick you up. I am very proud of you Jimmy; I always knew you would do well." With that Dean spun around and hopped back into his truck and motored out of the driveway.

After everything was cooked, Garth sat down to eat. The television was on but Garth was not really listening or watching. The announcer on the television was going on and on about the dry spring and how they were predicting poor crop production this year across the prairies due to below average rainfall forecasts. Garth's mind was elsewhere though as he munched away.

Garth finished his meal and began tidying up the dishes. As he was cleaning the last pot he saw his dad coming down the road with the tractor and air seeder. His dad pulled the machine around the grain bins and parked it, he let the machine idle down to cool off prior to turning it off. Jack climbed down the tractor and strolled across the yard towards the house.

Jack came through the door, and Garth could hear him rummaging around the landing as he removed his boots and hung his jacket. "Did you give that lady a call?" asked Jack. Jack usually didn't beat around the bush when it came to any conversation and especially with any that involved Garth. "Yes, I did, they are flying me out for an interview next week, I leave Tuesday, stay the night, meet with them on Wednesday and then come back later that day," explained Garth.

Garth got his dad's supper out for him and his dad sat down to eat. Garth told his dad all of the details of the phone call and of his itinerary. Jack listened intently, and then proceeded to give Garth advice on how he should act in the interview, what he should wear and even how he should answer their questions. Garth's eyes started to gloss over the more that Jack spoke. It was like this with Jack, always going into great details about how he should do this or don't do this. Garth found his dad to be constantly nagging at him, but Garth had learned to tune it out as he grew older. Sometimes, Garth didn't bother telling his dad certain things as he knew it would lead into another long discussion.

Garth changed the subject and said, "Uncle Dean stopped in and we are going into town tonight. Do you want to come with us?" asked Garth. "No, that's alright I am going to get to bed early tonight. Try not to be too late as I will need your help tomorrow. Be careful in town and don't drink too much. Be mindful of your uncle too, as he tends to get carried away," said Jack. Garth nodded and went to his room to get ready.

Dean was right on time and Garth hopped into Dean's truck. Dean gunned it and headed for Marley, which was about 11 miles away. As they drove along the narrow highway that led into Marley, Garth watched the endless fields pass by. Some had tractors pulling seeders and he could see the dust trails for miles around. The land was flat except for numerous small depressions in the fields that had been left behind when the glaciers receded over 10,000 years ago. These depressions or sloughs as they were called by the locals usually had water in the center, that would often dry up in the summer, and mixtures of willow and aspen growing on the edges.

Dean reached down below his seat and pulled out two bottles of Budweiser. "Here you go Jimmy," said Dean, "don't worry these are American beers, so it is basically water." Garth grabbed the bottle and twisted off the cap and took a long drink. Garth said, "you know Uncle that is a myth that Canadian beer has more alcohol than American beer." Dean shot him a glance of surprise and said, "what are you talking about?" Garth said, "the myth comes from measuring alcohol by different methods between the two countries. In Canada, the alcohol content is calculated by volume and in the States it is measured by weight. If the same calculation is applied, they basically have the same content."

Dean laughed and said, "Jimmy if there was ever a guy who was destined to be an engineer it was you. Who else would know that kind of shit?" Garth smiled and continued to look out the window at the chessboard pattern of the fields that passed and felt the rhythmic bumps of the frost heaved road.

"So, what did your dad have to say about the upcoming interview?" asked Dean. "I think he's pretty excited for me, but he spent most of the time telling me what to say and how to act in the interview. Sometimes I think he wants it more than I do."

"Well your dad really only wants the best for you," Dean said, "he just doesn't have a great way of showing it or saying it. I believe in you and I know deep down your dad does too."

Garth nodded and took another long swig of beer. As he was just about to finish the bottle the truck hit a large frost heave and he spilled beer down the front of his shirt. "Shit!" exclaimed Garth. His uncle laughed, "first day with a new mouth, Jimmy?" Garth just smiled and finished the rest of the beer as they passed the large green rectangular sign that indicated there was one kilometer to Marley.

Marley was a town of about 1,000 people and was situated at the confluence of three main highways and two railway lines. As many small towns had shrunk and disappeared over the years on the prairies, Marley had survived mainly due to the transportation links it boasted. Marley still had three wooden grain elevators which nowadays was rare for a town the size of Marley to have even one. At one time in Saskatchewan there were over 3,000 grain elevators and now there was less than 200, and Marley had three of them.

Garth had spent all thirteen years of school in Marley. His Grade twelve graduating class had only twelve graduates, of which nine were boys. This group had been together for most of the thirteen years, while some had moved away or dropped a grade. The majority of the them had grown up together from a young age. As unbelievable as this would seem in Jack's day none of his graduating class had stayed back in Marley. Some had gone on to University or College, but most had moved to the larger towns and cities and found work. It was rare anymore to find his friends back in Marley except around holidays.

As they drove through town, Garth admired the elm and oak trees that lined the streets. Most of the houses were at least thirty years old and the clear majority were bungalows.

Garth took notice of the houses as they passed as he knew who lived in most of the houses. He took a long glance at the quaint house that used to be home to a girl named Lauren who he had a crush on in elementary school. She had moved away with her Mom when she divorced her Dad. Her Dad still lived in the house but spent more time drinking now than anything else, which included any yardwork thought Garth as he eyed the rundown fence and unkempt grass that was littered with empty beer bottles and cases. Somehow, he always hoped he would see her outside there visiting her Dad.

Main Street held many old buildings and stores with false fronts, there was the pharmacy, grocery store, theatre and of course two Chinese restaurants, one on either side of the wide street. At the end of the street sat the Marley Hotel, which was a one story building that boasted a dozen rooms, a restaurant and lounge. As Dean, pulled into a vacant spot near the Hotel, Garth thought back to all of the hours and money he had spent in this establishment.

"Deano!" came a cry from the Hotel's main waitress, Coralee Russell, as soon as they entered. Coralee had been waitressing here ever since Garth was old enough to remember. She was about fifteen years older than Garth and she was attractive with long black hair. At one time, she and Dean had been a couple, but she eventually grew tired of Dean's indiscretions with other women in the neighboring towns. Coralee had married, had two boys and now was recently divorced. Garth could tell she still had deep feelings for Dean, and her cry of "Deano" had only solidified those thoughts.

"How are you boys today? Taking a break from the farming, are you?" asked Coralee. "We are here to have a few beers to celebrate as Jimmy here is going to be moving to the big city," said Dean. "We don't know that yet, Uncle," said Garth. "Okay, okay," laughed Dean, "but I think it is just a formality and you will soon be swinging with the big dicks in Calgary."

"Well congratulations Garth! We will certainly miss you around here," said Coralee. Garth just smiled in return. "So, I assume your usual. Two Budweisers?" asked Coralee. "You betcha," said Dean.

As Coralee turned to retrieve the beers from the bar, Garth noticed Dean checking out Coralee's rear view. Garth laughed to himself and continued to look around the lounge. There were about a dozen small round tables, one pool table and a small jukebox tucked in one corner. The place was empty except for three guys that Garth did not recognize playing pool. Garth assumed they must be oil patch workers. The only other patron was Phil McGregor: an old bachelor who could be found here on most nights drinking his life away. Garth nodded towards Phil but Phil did not return the nod.

Coralee returned to their table with the beers. "That will be seven dollars," she said. Dean pulled out his wallet and handed her a ten dollar bill. "Keep the change darling," he said. Dean and Garth sat for a few more rounds talking about the old times and the excitement for Garth with the future.

Garth's blood froze when a man sauntered into the lounge. He was a bulking man with a square head with a big black moustache. Oh, how Garth hated that moustache.

Garth's last years at the high school had not been his best. Garth had always been an A student but when a new principal had come to Marley when Garth was in Grade eleven, his marks plummeted. This principal's name was Cam Emery. Emery had taken the principal's job when the previous one retired. From day one Garth and Cam Emery had been at odds.

Emery in combination to being the principal also taught Physical Education, Biology and Social Studies. Garth was unsure what had instigated Emery's dislike for him, but Emery had been relentless in his bullying. For Physical Education, Emery would select teams to play different sports and always made sure he and Garth were on different sides. Emery would try to trip and shove Garth at every chance. In any class that Emery taught Garth he would make it a point to single out any mistake that Garth made and laugh about it with the other students.

Garth tried to distance himself as much as possible from Emery by dropping Social Studies and Biology. This pained Garth very much as Biology was one of his favorite studies. In fact, if it wasn't for Emery, Garth may have chosen a different career in Agriculture. However, since Biology was a prerequisite for Agriculture studies in University, Garth had selected Engineering as his career path instead.

Garth had never known what it was like to be bullied until Emery came to town. It made Garth sick with the hypocrisy as teachers like Emery would show support behind anti-bullying campaigns when they were the worst culprits.

Now Emery and his black moustache had entered the lounge and his eyes now settled on Garth and Dean. "So, what do we owe the pleasure of having two Gibbins boys in the bar tonight?" bellowed Emery.

"Hello Cam," said Dean, "Garth here is going to be moving to Calgary, and work for an oil company," said Dean. "So, you have a job already," said Emery as his blood shot black eyes burned into Garth's. It was still early in the evening but Garth could tell that Emery was well lubricated. In a cracked voice, Garth replied "I am flying out there for an interview next week." "Celebrating a little early, aren't you? I mean they haven't even seen your carcass yet and you think they are going to just hand you a job?" sneered Emery.

Dean said, "they are flying him all the way out there and they don't just do that for anyone. We are going to celebrate what we want to celebrate, regardless of what you think."

"Fine Dean, fine, well than at least let me buy you a round of beers," said Emery. "Coralee. Bring two more Budweisers for these guys and I will have a double rye and coke," said Emery.

"Thank you, Cam," said Dean. "Now if you guys will excuse me, I have to piss my dink," said Dean as he rose. Emery slid a chair over to their table and sat down. Coralee brought the drinks over and Emery took a big drink of his. He opened his mouth and savoured the drink. He leaned in and looked at Garth.

"Well, I guess you will be the hero of the town now. A big shot engineer in the big city. But remember this, your uncle won't always be there to protect you and you won't be missed at all in this town. Hell, even your own mother doesn't care that you exist," said Emery.

Before he knew what he was doing Garth sprung out of his chair, sending it flying backwards. He cocked his arm and threw a right cross that landed squarely on Emery's left eye. It was the hardest that Garth had ever struck another human being. Unfortunately for Garth it did not have the effect he thought it would. This is what Emery had been waiting for. He countered Garth's offering with a right cross of his own that connected with Garth's nose. Garth saw a flood of stars and had the iron taste of blood in his mouth. He crumpled to the floor. Emery was about to climb on top of Garth to finish the job when Dean exited the bathroom at a dead run. Dean reached out and grabbed the greasy black hair on the top of Emery's head and as he tilted his head back, Dean smashed one of the full bottles of beer across his head. This stunned the drunken Emery and as he turned his head Dean landed a punch to his nose. The unmistakable and disgusting sound of bone breaking could be heard throughout the bar and Emery fell to the ground with his face splattered with blood.

Coralee screamed, "Dean. No!" Dean let Emery fall to the floor. "I told you before to leave him alone, you son of a bitch," yelled Dean. Emery just lay moaning where he fell. "I am sorry Coralee, but this has been a long time coming, "said Dean. Dean grabbed Garth and looked at his face. There was a red mark on his nose and he was probably going to have black eyes but nothing looked to be broken. "Come on, let's get out of here," said Dean.

"That's it! Get out of here both of you," screamed Emery still holding his nose and bleeding all over that stupid bushy moustache. "Oh, just shut up Cam. You have done enough," said Coralee, as she handed him a cloth for his nose.

As they headed towards the truck, Dean said, "what was that all about?" "Sorry Uncle, but he has been a thorn in my side ever since he came here and when he said how even my own mother wants nothing to do with me, I lost it," said Garth. Garth's heart was racing and he was so angry that he could feel tears welling up.

"All I can say is nice shot but next time you have to be quick to follow up with another, as one usually isn't enough. And when you are faced with an asshole like that once you knock him down, never let him back up," said Dean.

Dean and Garth climbed into Dean's truck. Both of their right hands were still stinging. Garth enjoyed that warm pain in his hand. The one in his nose not so much.

Dean said, "I am proud of you for standing up for yourself. Always stick to what you believe and stand up for yourself and people will respect that. You will do great in Calgary, but always stick to your guns."

"You are too good for this town anyways," said Dean, "being here will always drag you down." "How can you say that Uncle? The people here absolutely love you," said Garth. "Do you think they would love me if I had made it as a professional hockey player, though?" asked Dean, "I don't. Small towns can be finicky, people will bond with people that are like them, people who have tried and failed. Some people get jealous if they see another succeed where they didn't. Rather than embrace it and be happy for the person, they will resort to bashing him, saying he was a drunk, stuck up or anything. Now I am not saying everyone is like that, but it is more noticeable in a small town. You know Brad Bergeron from Wolf Creek who plays with the Edmonton Oilers?" Garth nodded. Dean said, "well most people in that town will say that he wasn't talented and how his parents paid his way, and that he was an arrogant trouble making kid that was always up to no good in the town. They may have a sign up outside of town saying "Home of Brad Bergeron" but that's as far as it goes. Instead of being truly proud of him, the town in a way resented him. I played against him and I can tell you he was a great kid but most parents hated him, called him a "puck hog" or were mad at him because their kid didn't get to play with Brad eating up most of the ice time. Marley tolerates me because I was good but never made it anywhere. I don't remind them of how their lives and dreams didn't work out."

They drove in silence and when they were a couple of miles out of town, Dean turned to Garth and said, "You know how everybody says that the best view of Marley is from cemetery hill as the sun is going down." "Yeah," said Garth. "Well look here," said Dean as he pointed to the rear-view mirror. "That is the best view of Marley right here and never look back."

Chapter 2

It was 7:30 AM, as the electric light rail transit train moved along the track. Many months had passed since the unfortunate events at the Marley hotel. Garth was a Reservoir Engineer now for Maldere's natural gas properties on the Southern Alberta Team. As Reservoir Engineer, he was responsible for production forecasting, reserve bookings, well development plans and budgeting of the property. It was a responsibility that he enjoyed as it was similar to being the quarterback on a football team.

The train swayed and jerked back and forth as it made its way towards the tall buildings of downtown Calgary. The city was covered with a brown haze that hung close to the ground. The haze contrasted with the bright blue sky that surrounded the landscape of the rolling hills, trees and roof tops of the city. Garth moved back and forth with the rhythm of the train as he stood in one of the aisles hanging onto a handle that hung from the ceiling. The train was packed. Some people were like him headed to their downtown high rise office jobs. These people were easy to spot; they were well dressed, some with suits and ties and some dressed in "business casual" which was pressed pants with a polo shirt or something similar, except on Fridays when most companies allowed their employees to wear blue jeans. There were students heading to classes, construction workers, and homeless people as well. Garth was always amazed by the huge variety of people that frequented the train every day.

The train pulled into a stop and the digital voice came over the intercom and said, "Center Street Station". Garth chuckled every time he heard the digitized woman's voice as it sounded as if the recording was playing back at three times the normal speed. Garth waited for the people to empty before he exited. Garth hated how people acted when the train doors opened, as some people would trample over one another to get off and people would try to get on without letting the people off first. Garth always hesitated till the last to avoid these people.

Garth saw a white-haired man coming towards him in dirty clothes and unkempt hair who was asking the people leaving the train for money. This same fellow was always there and would try to strike up a conversation with Garth about some crazed conspiracy theories. Garth saw a chance to avoid this fellow, so he lagged behind a group of construction workers then fell in behind two female college students.

Garth then went around the corner and walked down the street to the Tim Hortons coffee shop on 8th Avenue across from his office. It was a normal weekly ritual for him and four of his colleagues to meet for coffee at this location prior to work on Friday mornings. However, since Friday of this week was a holiday they had decided to meet this morning.

As usual, Garth was the first one there. There were ten people in front of him at the order line up. Garth knew the orders for his co-workers by heart. Two of them currently worked with Garth on the Southern Alberta Team, Mike Baxter was the Production Engineer and Brady Bennet was the Geologist.

As Garth waited, he looked over his shoulder and saw a man approaching who was well over six feet, broad shoulders and a thick moustache. This was Ken McAdam, who was a Geologist that had previously worked with the three of them but had since been assigned to the Northeast British Columbia team. "G squared," exclaimed Ken, "how are you this morning?" Garth said, "just fine! How are you Ken?" "My ex-wife has been riding my ass like a rodeo cowboy, but other than that bitch I guess things are fine," said Ken in a big booming voice. Ken was prone to making off the cuff remarks such as this that would make Garth feel uncomfortable. Garth turned his head away and saw that some of the other patrons were now looking at them. Some with supreme annoyance and one anyways of an older man in the corner who gave a nod, as if to say, "I hear you, man".

As Garth and Ken at one time had offices right next to each other, Garth had overheard a lot of the conversations between Ken and his ex-wife. Therefore, he had gotten the one-sided view from Ken on a daily basis, which was way more information than anyone ever needed.

Mike and Brady came through the door together. "Good morning ladies," said Ken as they walked up to Garth and Ken. "Grab us a table and I think it is my turn to get coffee this morning," said Ken. Garth stayed in line to help Ken with the order as Mike and Brady grabbed a table over by the window.

Five minutes later with coffees in hand, Garth and Ken took their places at the table. The talk was casual as always, talking about the week that was and the weekend coming up. Ken normally would say something that would throw the three of them into fits of laughter. Garth was always amazed by his witty remarks and every week he would have new ones.

Amid the laughter, Ken straight faced turned to Garth and said, "hey, you know Russ McConnell who is the Reservoir Engineer for the Northeast British Columbia team?" Garth said, "sure he was the one that got hammered at the Christmas party last year and was making out with the Human Resources lady." "Yep that's him. He handed in his notice yesterday and he is moving on to a smaller company, called Huntoon Oil and Gas or something like that. Anyways there is going to be an opening to replace him and you should put your name in. You have been under Ralph long enough and the properties in Northeast B.C. are similar to what you have been working on with the gas in South Alberta. I think it would be a good fit for you." "I don't know they usually want pretty senior guys for that," replied Garth. Ken smiled at said, "you have to take a chance, Columbus took a chance and look at what he discovered." The others laughed at this remark from Ken.

Garth smiled and said, "you know Columbus based his "chance" on incorrect math. He miscalculated a degree of latitude and underestimated the circumference of earth by about 35%. He certainly would have killed everyone trying to sail to Asia but lucked out by hitting land in the Caribbean. He was so sure he had calculated correctly that even until he died, he believed he had landed in Asia." "I thought everyone thought the world was flat and Columbus proved them wrong?" said Brady. "Actually, at that time most everyone knew the world was round, they just didn't know that the Americas were there. No one had sailed to Asia because in the day they knew it was too far for a ship of the day to make it. They couldn't carry enough fresh water for everyone. That is why Portugal didn't support Columbus because they knew his math was wrong", said Garth.

"Where do you get all this stuff from?" said Mike. Garth said, "you know those Worldbook encyclopedias they used to sell. Well my dad bought them and I read most of them from cover to cover when there was nothing else to do on the farm. We had peasant vision on tv, which meant we had 3 channels and 2 were the same." "Geez you must have been a real party animal back in Marley!", laughed Ken.

"You are just as crazy as Columbus then and you should still take the chance at the North East B.C. job anyways", said Ken. "Okay, okay I will bring it up with Ralph", conceded Garth.

After they had finished up their coffee, they made the trek back to their offices. They entered the Maldere building and walked to the elevators, it was just after 8 am as they entered the elevator. Mike, Brady and Garth got off on the twelfth floor and said their goodbyes to Ken as he continued his ride up to his office on fourteen.

Mike was the first one off of the elevator and went towards the glass doors that were the main entrance to the floor. He pulled out his plastic security card and ran it over the card reader that was outside the door. There was a metallic click as the magnets holding the door released and Mike pulled the right door open and held it open for Garth and Brady as they walked through.

The three of them said their "have a good day" and went their separate ways. Mike and Brady went down the hallway to the left and Garth continued on down the right. The Maldere building had its offices set up in a ring around the outside corridor of the building. There were offices on the outside and inside, the outside offices had windows to the outside of the building and the offices with a mountain view were highly coveted. The inside offices had no windows and were typically relegated to the "support staff" which included production accountants, engineering technicians and geological assistants. The outside offices were left for the "professional staff" which included the geologists, engineers and landmen. The outside corner offices also had much larger floor plans and were saved for the managers. There was one manager for Geology, Reservoir Engineering, Production Engineering and Land.

Garth walked down the hallway towards his office. The outside offices had glass walls that had frosting on them to allow some privacy but one could still tell if the occupant was in their office as one walked by. Each office also had a number outside of it and the name of the occupant. The offices were set up in teams, meaning that the production engineer, reservoir engineer, geologist and landmen for each team were next to one another to instigate and assist with communication. Garth would say "good morning" to anyone he saw in their office. The hallways were decorated with various paintings that reminded Garth of cheap Hotel artwork. The artwork would change periodically, and Garth surmised that was to return them to the Hotel from whence they came. The carpet on this floor had a design that reminded Garth of the game Pick Up Sticks with sticks of alternating blue, green, red and yellow on a dark grey background. Garth was told once that it represented when working in an office how everyone and everything is connected. Garth had rolled his eyes when he was told this because all he saw was a shitty looking carpet that made his eyes hurt if he looked at it for too long.

Garth's office was an outside office that was right next to a corner office that belonged to Dave Piett the Reservoir Manager for the Southern Alberta team. Dave Piett had been with the company since Maldere Energy had been founded by Roger Maldere over 20 years ago. Dave Piett was a man of a small stature and small face that was hidden by an immaculate beard. Behind his back the other employees referred to him as Big Dave, this was a tongue-in-cheek reference to his small size. But what Dave Piett lacked in the way of physical appearance he more than made up for in his no non-sense attitude and ability to play the games of the political landscape in Maldere Energy.

Garth found any conversation with Dave uncomfortable. Dave's cold grey eyes seemed to penetrate right through his very soul when he was conversing and Garth would struggle to communicate effectively with him. This morning as Garth walked by his office, he could see Dave was sitting at his desk facing the door. Garth sighed. There was no way to avoid him this morning. Garth quickened his pace and said, "good morning Dave." But before Garth could make his door, the words "Garth, good morning. Do you have a moment?" stopped him in his tracks.

"You bet," said Garth. Garth turned and entered Piett's office. His office was probably twice as large as Garth's and along with the normal computer desk and office chair, Piett's office had a circular table surrounded with four leather backed office chairs. "Close the door," said Dave.

As Garth turned back towards the center of the office, Dave motioned for him to take a seat at the round table. Garth sat down and Dave grabbed a bunch of printouts from his desk and took his place at the table next to Garth. "I have been waiting for you this morning but I guess today must be Tim Horton's day," smirked Dave. Garth was caught off guard by the comment and found himself unable to respond, but Dave seemed to take pleasure from the blank look on Garth's face. "Don't worry. I am sure you will make up the time," said Dave.

Dave took the printouts and placed them in front of Garth. Garth recognized them immediately. He had prepared them for Ralph when he was asked to do an infill drilling evaluation of the Second White Specks formation in the Alderson area of Southern Alberta.

"I understand you prepared this evaluation?" said Dave. "Yes, I did," said Garth. "Alright, I just wanted to go over a few things with you if I could and provide you with some suggestions," said Dave. "First off, I noticed that you have not included any decline analysis graphs. I am not sure how you can do an analysis of any field without them"

Garth cringed at this comment. Decline analysis was a method that is widely used by most engineers for estimating reserves that a gas or oil well will produce. It is a graphical method that involves fitting a best fit line through actual production data and then assuming the well will continue to produce at the same decline rate until the end of its producing life.

Garth remembered back to his classes where his Reservoir Engineering instructor had taught him that most people used and abused decline analysis because it was too easy to use. "Any preschooler with crayons can do decline analysis," was what he used to say. He had pounded it into Garth that decline analysis was a tool but it told you nothing about the reservoir, and a poor Reservoir Engineer would rely on it exclusively.

"I have developed my own evaluation program in a spreadsheet that can handle transient and boundary dominated flow," replied Garth, "the reason I did this is that these wells remain in transient for about year and for most of the newer wells I have only 1 or 2 years of production data to analyze. For these reasons, the decline analysis is not valid."

Dave looked directly at Garth and said, "so you created your own method that you can manipulate the data to give any answers that you want?" Garth cringed and said, "no, I have used both transient and boundary dominated formulas that are widely accepted. I then combined them with material balance to predict the reservoir pressure at each match point." "Material balance doesn't work for this type of wells," snapped Dave.

"In my model, I make an assumption on the original gas in place and use the material balance equation to estimate the reservoir pressure as the gas depletes. This reservoir pressure is then used in the flow formulas to give an estimate of the gas rate for each time step. I use this to match the historical production of the well. From this model, I can get a better picture of the reservoir such as permeability and pressure. This allows me to give a better estimation of how the wells will perform," said Garth. Garth's heart was beating a mile a minute and he could feel himself starting to sweat. Garth always felt insecure in these types of exchanges and right now he was wishing this would end soon.

Garth could see the look on Dave's face, and could detect the slightest of a smirk. The look reminded Garth of the look that Cam Emery would have when he was berating Garth in front of the class back in high school. Dave could smell blood in the water as he saw how this was making Garth uncomfortable and was enjoying grilling this greenhorn.

"I am going to caution you on taking this analysis any further," Dave said, "you are now combining many unknowns in your spreadsheet or your so called "model". I have been doing reservoir engineering in these tight gas plays for a lot of years, so you can take this as a learning experience. You need to group the wells by the year they have been drilled and at what spacing and conduct decline analysis on them. From these reserves estimates you can predict what can be done in the future. From your analysis, you have greatly underestimated the gas in place and are saying there is only room to drill 4 wells per 640 acres for the Second White Specks. These reservoirs are different and the conventional type of analysis you are doing does not apply and will give erroneous results. I know there is enough gas here that we can drill at least 16 wells. So, go back and reanalyze this."

At this, Garth took his chance to put this conversation to an end. "Thank you, I will Dave," said Garth. Dave smiled his repulsive grin and said, "good." With that Garth went to his office and closed his door and sat at his desk. He was turning the conversation over and over in his head and there were so many other responses that he wanted to give to explain himself but he knew it was useless. What was done was done.

A tap came to the door and Garth could see through the frosted glass that it was Ralph Hill his Reservoir Engineering mentor. Ralph was about 10 years older than Garth and worked all of his engineering career at Maldere. Garth often thought that if one was to look up what an engineer should look like in a book they would find a picture of Ralph Hill, minus the pocket protector.

Garth said, "come in." With that the handle turned and Ralph entered into the office and took a seat in one of the guest chairs. Ralph whispered, "I see that Dave had you in his office. Was it about your analysis of the infill program?" "Yes," replied Garth, "he said I need to work on it more and that my conclusions are not justified."

Ralph continued, "Dave had come to me first and I had mentioned that you were working on it and you were using more traditional methods rather than just decline analysis. He got worked up about that and said he would talk to you direct. I hope everything went okay." Garth studied Ralph for a moment, he could see that Ralph was flushed and uncomfortable. Ralph was a nice enough guy and good engineer but even more than Garth he hated confrontation. Garth knew enough about Ralph to know that he was not going to back him when push came to shove.

"I'll get him the decline analysis he's looking for and I am sure it will be fine, thanks," replied Garth. "Are you going to hockey at lunch hour?" Garth asked. "You bet," said Ralph, "I talked to a bunch of the other guys so we should have a good turnout. If you need any help with the infill review let me know." "I will, thanks," said Garth.

Ralph got up out of the chair and left Garth's office. Garth fired up his computer. Thoughts were rolling through his head on how he was going to get this project together for Dave. He knew that Ralph would try to help him but he liked doing these types of things on his own.

Garth reviewed his e-mail once the computer started up. There were fifteen new e-mails, but none of them were really work related. Most of the e-mails referred to an upcoming event for a fun casino that the company social club was putting on. Garth chuckled at some of the other e-mails where people would respond that they were going by hitting the reply all button rather than just replying to the event coordinator. After deleting the e-mails, Garth set to work on updating his analysis, and reluctantly incorporate the decline analysis that Big Dave asked for.

Garth managed to work diligently on this project for the rest of the morning uninterrupted. He gathered up the most recent production information and proceeded to send the graphs to the closest of the two printers on the floor.

Garth hated sending his material to these printers as many people liked to amuse themselves by snooping and reading other people's material. Garth quickly got up and headed for the printer as soon as he hit print.

Garth rounded the corner and stepped into the copy room. He was instantly hit with a wall of sickening body odor. He knew immediately "Stinky Pete" had recently been there. Stinky Pete's real name was Peter Bozak. He was a fellow Reservoir Engineer that worked in a different area than Garth.

Garth leafed through the printouts sitting on the deck of the printer. There were some pages dedicated to the coverups of climate change and he knew those belonged to Stinky Pete. As Garth grabbed his printouts turning to leave, he heard a squealy voice say, "Hello Garth". "Hello Pete," said Garth, "how are you today?" Pete smiled a toothy grin and said, "just fine, thanks. Have you seen the latest comments by our fear-less Prime Minister on global warming?"

"No sorry. I haven't," replied Garth. Garth sighed he really did not want to get into a debate on this subject, or any subject for that matter with Pete. "He says that human-made climate change is a hoax, created by Asian countries to make the rest of the world uncompetitive," said Pete, "I can't believe people still don't believe in global warming." Pointing to the pile of papers on the printer, Garth shrugged, "never be surprised by what people believe. For instance. I can't believe people think that printing this stuff out is a good use of Company time." Garth shook his head and left Pete standing there with a blank look on his face.

Garth placed the printouts on his desk and proceeded to leaf through them and organize them into piles that he would later put into binders. One thing that bothered Garth was a cluttered desk and he liked to keep everything organized.

Garth was working away diligently when he could hear a loud but friendly voice coming down the hallway. The voice was telling jokes and laughing all the way down the hall. Garth looked at his watch. It was now just after 11 am and Ken McAdams was making his way to Garth's office to give him a ride to hockey.

"Gibbers!", said Ken as he walked into Garth's office. "Stop pretending you're working and let's roll. We need you at tip top mental capacity for this game today. We're playing first place Prowse Drilling, so you better be ready to skate your ass off."

"I am just finishing this up, will only take a moment", said Garth. "Forget that shit and let's go," said Ken, "unlike my ex-wife, the nice thing about work is that it will always be there for you."

Garth usually caught a ride with Ken for the weekly lunch-time hockey. As Garth's place was on the way, Ken would stop at Garth's for Garth to grab his hockey equipment. This worked out great for Garth as it was a huge pain in the ass to have to take his hockey equipment on the LRT.

A tall blonde-haired man was standing by Ken's Mustang. Garth recognized him as Darcy Lowe. Darcy was a Completions Engineer and a heck of a hockey player. He did not make it out very often to hockey but when he did Garth enjoyed playing on a line with him. Darcy was talented but seemed to enjoy setting people up rather than doing the scoring himself. Garth was not the best skater but one thing he did have was a great scoring touch and Darcy seemed to really enjoy feeding him the puck.

"Hi Darcy," said Garth, "good to see you can make it out today." "Wouldn't miss it," said Darcy, "I know a lot of those guys on the Prowse team, and they've been talking smack all week. I would enjoy nothing better than shutting them up."

They climbed into the Mustang. It was a bit cramped with the three grown men and two hockey bags with another bag yet to come. Ken turned the key and the 5.0-liter engine fired up to life. The car was not new by any stretch and even though Ken had money to buy a new one he still hung on to this car. Garth figured that it was probably due to Ken wanting to hang on to his youth and this car represented a huge part of it.

When the car started, the music that Ken was last listening to came on full blast. Garth jumped a little as the music blared up. Ken quickly turned the music down to more of a manageable level. "Well nothing like showing your age, driving this old Pedophile vehicle and cranking Fleetwood Mac," laughed Darcy. "Careful Darce. You can knock my car but lay off of Stevie. She still has the sexiest, raspy voice I have ever heard" replied Ken.

Ken then spun the tires and sped out of the parkade. He headed down the one-way street and up the Center Street bridge over the Bow River to Garth's place. Ken parked the car on the street and Garth ran up to collect his hockey equipment.

When Garth returned to the car, Darcy turned to him and asked, how is work going with Big Dave?" "Shitty," said Garth. "He's got me doing some production and pressure testing on some wells," said Darcy, "I guess the pressures weren't showing him what he wanted. He is blaming me for screwing up the pressures somehow." Garth said, "I didn't know they were doing any work like that. What was wrong with the pressures?"

"The pressures were supposed to build up to initial pressure. Instead of doing that all of them are showing declining pressures," said Darcy. "The pressures are showing interference," said Garth, "I knew it. The wells are too close to each other." Darcy nodded. "Big Dave is upset because that is the last thing he wants and doesn't want to believe that is happening. They have hundreds of wells planned and this would put them in jeopardy," said Darcy.

"And that bastard is making me redo all my work," said Garth, "those declining pressures prove that my theory on the infill drilling is right. It is primarily accelerating production rather than adding new reserves. Would you be able to send me that pressure data?" "Gladly," said Darcy, "come down to my office when we get back after the game. Now use some of that anger against Prowse today and we should thump them."

They arrived at the Edwards Arena and exited the car. Garth was the first one to the arena door and held it open for Ken and Darcy. Aside from them, the atrium was empty. Garth glanced at the bulletin board and saw that the Maldere Marauders were in dressing room two. The three of them headed down the hallway. The dressing rooms were located in a hallway that ran beside the ice rink where the Zamboni was just finishing up in resurfacing the ice.

They could hear the music blaring further down the hall from dressing room four where their opponents were getting ready. The trio opened the door to their dressing room and entered. Garth inhaled the distinctive smell that accompanies any hockey rink. It is a smell that Garth was sure is the bane to most hockey moms. Garth had found it difficult to explain the smell to someone who had not been to a hockey rink. The smell was not as simple as body odor, it was kind of sweet smelling but overpowering that combined the odor of a wet horse with human sweat and ammonia. To Garth it was a familiar comforting smell that smelled like, well fun.

Garth looked around the room at the usual skaters. It was perfect. There would be two full lines plus Norm Davis, the goalie. Norm did not work at Maldere and was a Salesman that worked for a pipeline supplier. As it was usually hard to find someone that had goalie equipment, teams were allowed to look outside the company for a goalie. The other observation he made was that that Tyler Henderson was not there. Tyler was also a Reservoir Engineer and about the same age as Garth. Tyler seemed to relish competing with Garth whether it was at work or play. All it did was annoy Garth as Tyler would constantly chirp as he knew it got to Garth.

Garth had come to realize that he could tell a lot about how most people were to work with at the office by how they played hockey. Really when someone is on a team in the office it is not dissimilar to being on a team in hockey. Uncle Dean had told Garth that sports build character. Garth had found it more fitting to say that sports, like wine, brings out one's true character. In Garth's mind, the person who typified this observation, was Tyler Henderson.

The talk around the dressing room was light and good natured as the guys put their hockey equipment on. Soon the talk centered on Ken's base layers that he wore to every game. Tattered and worn jock shorts that Garth swore were 20 years old and a Fleetwood Mac cotton t-shirt that sported a young Stevie Nicks in a black top hat on the front. The image on the front was faded and the shirt had quite a few tears and just as many stains. Ken said it was lucky for him as the first time he had worn the ensemble he had scored a hat trick.

"Hey Ken," said Garth, "if you score a hat trick today, I will order you a new shirt off E-bay." The chatter then turned to a crescendo of cackles and cat calls as Ken always played defense. He was a stay at home defensemen who rarely scored many goals. At the height of their fun at Ken's expense, the door opened and in popped Tyler Henderson.

The room fell silent as Tyler walked in. Except for the usual "hi Henders" or "how is it going, Tyler". Garth thought, "*shit.*" Instead of having six forwards they would now have seven. This made it hard to juggle to ensure everyone got equal playing time.

Garth quickly dressed and headed out on the ice. He did not feel comfortable having to sit in the room and strike up a conversation with Tyler. He knew that eventually the discussion would turn to work and Tyler of course would know the best way to do everything and that the way that Garth did things was wrong.

The Zamboni had finished and the ice was still wet in a few spots when Garth skated out. Garth was the first one out from his team and soon the whole Drillers team was out on the ice with him. Garth skated over to one side of the boards to do his stretches and watched the Drillers go through their warm up at the other end of the rink.

Soon the rest of the Marauders skated out on the ice and they went through their pre game warm up. After about five minutes of warm up, the referee skated out. Ken called all of the players over to the player's bench. Ken was the relegated captain for the team. "Aidan and Nathan will start on defense and Darcy, Ryan and Henders can be the first forwards. We will go with five defense today. Garth, Curt and Pat will be the other forwards. Myself, Tim and Gord will be on D." Nobody said a word and nodded their heads.

Garth skated to the bench. He was disappointed, as this meant he would not get to play with Darcy. Garth would be playing with Curt and Pat. Pat was okay to play with but Curt was a real puck hog. He would skate himself into a corner and lose the puck rather than try to pass the puck to a teammate. This was frustrating to Garth but he had learned a way to deal with guys like that.

The players took their positions at center ice and the referee dropped the puck. Darcy was playing center and cleanly won the face off over to Tyler. Tyler made a move around the closest defender but had the puck knocked off of his stick by a towering defenseman.

The play started out back and forth with no side really able to develop a quality scoring chance. After about a minute, Darcy and Ryan came to the bench for their line change but Tyler stayed on the ice. Tyler was playing left wing which was Garth's position but would not come off.

Thirty seconds later when the whistle finally blew, Tyler slowly skated to the bench with a sheepish grin on his face. Garth with a scowl on his skated onto the ice past him without saying a word.

The puck was dropped in the Marauder's defensive zone. Curt won the faceoff through the opposing player's legs and picked up the puck and headed into the neutral zone. Garth accelerated around the player covering him and they skated into the Driller's zone on a two on two. Garth had played enough with Curt to know that he was not going to get a pass from him. As they crossed the blue line, he positioned himself behind Curt. Garth was going to get a rebound from Curt's shot. Or he would pick the puck up while Curt floundered and lost the puck when he tried to split the Defense on his own.

Curt had the puck poke checked away from him easily by one of the Driller's defensemen. The puck rolled on edge towards the right wing corner and Garth pounced on it. Garth gave a quick glance over his shoulder and saw Pat crossing the blue line headed to the net. Pat was all alone as the other Driller's players were focused on the puck in the corner. He fed a beautiful pass to Pat. Garth then went to the net. He did not see that his pass was right on the money but Pat did not have his stick on the ice and missed the pass cleanly. The puck hit the far boards and a Driller player who was dogging it back into his own zone picked up the loose puck and accelerated back towards the Marauder's zone on a clear breakaway. The Driller came in at full speed from his strong side and tried to make a deke to get Norm to move and open up a hole between his legs. However, when Norm slid across the blade of his goalie stick became caught up between his legs and the puck hit the stick. When Norm felt this, he squeezed his legs and was able to cover the puck and keep it out of the net.

As Garth skated passed the bench to get in position for the face off in their end, Tyler yelled out, "hey Gibbins be sure of that pass, that almost cost us. You should have gone wide and gave Curt someone to pass to." Garth was fuming and thought to himself, *"yeah like I was going to get a pass from Curt. If Pat had picked up that pass we could have scored."* Garth only glared back at Tyler. Let the bastard chirp. The rest of the team knew Garth had made the right choice.

Garth watched from the bench as Tyler cut across the ice from his left wing position. He got in behind the defenseman and gobbled up the loose puck and skated it towards the Driller's net. Tyler took a quick wrister that he rifled over the goalie's shoulder on the short side. The shot was perfect and the Marauder's had the first goal of the game. The Marauder's bench jumped up to celebrate. "What a shot", said Gord. Garth nodded his head, although he didn't like it. He did have to admit that was a hell of a shot.

On Garth's next shift, Pat executed a beautiful behind the back no look pass right onto his stick. He skated in alone on the goalie and snapped a wrist shot towards the net. He fanned on the shot but the puck was able to sneak through the goalie's legs and trickled across the goal line. It was now 2-0.

Garth celebrated with his line and then skated to the bench. The first words he heard were that of Tyler. "You sure got all of that one", said Tyler sarcastically, "that barely made it across."

"They all count", interjected Darcy. Garth took his place on the bench, even though they were winning, he was mad as hell.

The score grew to 4-0 and Garth found his line with an offensive zone faceoff. Curt won the faceoff to Pat, who skated with the puck behind the net. Garth positioned himself to the right of the net with a Driller's defensemen right on him. Pat came around the net and fired a hard pass to Garth. Garth had his stick off the ice jostling for position with the defensemen and the pass went through his legs. The puck glanced off the side boards right onto the stick of the Driller's left winger. He skated the puck to center ice and he had a clear breakaway in on Norm. The Driller player tried to deke Norm to his glove side but Norm stood his ground and made a nice pad save that was cleared by the Marauder's defense down the ice for an icing call.

As Garth skated off the ice, Tyler skated passed him and snarled," Gibbins keep your stick on the ice. That one is on you." Garth could feel his face turning red as the anger welled up inside of him. Pat skated up beside Garth and said, "sorry man. That pass had a little too much heat on it. Nice back check though. I thought you were going to catch that guy."

With the score still 4-0 the Drillers finally caught a break when a tired Tyler coughed up the puck to give them an odd man rush. Tyler slowly skated to the bench. When he finally got close enough, Garth bolted for the other end of the ice to try to break up the play. He quickly gained speed and caught up to one of the forwards without the puck. He lifted his stick to disrupt the player's ability to accept a pass if one came. The puck carrier cut back and circled to the front of the net. He was too far forward to stop this. He tried to poke check the player but lost his edge and fell on his backside. He fell into the crease and blocked Norm from getting over to the side of the net to block the shot. The Driller's player made an easy backhand into the open side of the net and the Driller's had their first goal.

Garth laid on the ice for a moment then picked himself up and said, "sorry, Normy." Norm just looked at him and shook his head. As the players skated back to center ice for the face off, Tyler leaned over the boards and yelled, "Gibbins if you could stay off your ass maybe you could have stopped that one. Come on. Get your head into the game."

Garth's face flashed red again. Garth thought about skating over there with a smile on his face and punching him in the face. He thought to himself the arrogant little bastard would never even know it was coming. Before anything could escalate, Ken stepped in and said "Hey Henders, why don't you give your mouth a rest for a while. If you skated as fast as you run your mouth you would have been a fucking NHL superstar."

Tyler just looked at Ken and said nothing. Garth was surprised that Tyler didn't have a snappy come back for that. But that was usually the way it goes with bullies, once they get challenged by someone they quickly back down.

The game continued. Both teams scored one more goal each, making the final score 5-2. After the teams had exchanged the customary handshakes at the end of the game the players headed to their dressing rooms.

"Good game boys", said Ken. "Norm, what the hell? Whatever you had for breakfast have it again before the next game. Awesome job. Hey guys, I have a box at the Dome tonight for the Flames and Sharks game from one of our Drilling company reps. There is room for six guys."

Garth waited to hear what the other players said before making his availability known. There was no way he was going if Tyler was. He had seen enough of that son of a bitch for a while. "Sorry guys, but I have a date with Cathleen Leslie tonight", said Tyler. Garth was glad that Tyler wasn't going but he was surprised and a little jealous that Cathleen was dating

Tyler. Garth knew Cathleen from work. She was a Geologist for the Northwest Alberta team and too good for the likes of Tyler.

"Gibbers, you coming?" asked Ken. "You bet, sounds good", replied Garth. He couldn't help thinking about Cathleen with Tyler. Garth was a sucker for a red-headed woman and the first time he glanced into her eyes, Garth felt a mutual attraction. He had felt mutual attractions with women before but never that strong. Garth, being too shy, had never followed it up and now here she was going on a date with that asshole Tyler.

Chapter 3

Garth's thoughts were consumed with Tyler rather than work. He was at his desk but only in body and not in mind. Ken materialized in the doorway after what seemed an eternity. "Come on Gibbers," said Ken, "time to clock out. We are going to Johnny's Old Towne Tavern for some grub and suds first. We will meet the rest of the crew there and grab some cabs to the Saddledome."

At the pub, Garth started to come around. The other four guys that were going to the game were Pat, Curt, Nathan and Aidan. They were all guys that Garth liked. Garth had been to a couple of Flames games before, but in the nosebleed section. This would be the first time he would be sitting in the box seats.

When the cab dropped Garth off at the foot of the steps up to the Saddledome there were many fans milling about. Most were dressed in Flames jerseys but there were a few sporting the San Jose Sharks colors. Before they walked into the main concourse Ken led them down the stairs that led to the luxury seats.

Down the stairs was a huge area with tables, chairs and a large bar. The floors were carpeted unlike the cement floors on the main levels. *So, this is how the other half lives,* thought Garth. Ken noted the expression on Garth's face. "You won't want to go to another game on the main level now," said Ken, "it's kind of like going back to gen pop at a prison, compared to this." Garth said nothing and nodded as he stood taking it all in.

"There he is," said Ken. Garth's eyes followed Ken's and he saw a small balding man wearing an Iginla jersey coming towards them with his hand extended. The man introduced himself as Mark who was the Account Manager for Executrix Drilling. "Thanks for coming guys," said Mark, "I would like to introduce you to my other guests from Huntoon Oil and Gas. I don't usually do this. But since Russ used to work with you and Ken said it was okay. I thought I would invite them to join us."

Behind Mark were five people. Garth recognized Russ McConnell right away and said hello and shook his hand. When Russ turned away, Garth could see the other four people behind him. Three men came up to introduce themselves. As soon as they said their names Garth had forgotten them. His attention was on the fourth person. She wore white sneakers, blue jeans and her flowing Strawberry blonde hair draped over the shoulders of her San Jose jersey.

"Hi, Michelle Newfield. Nice to meet you," she said. Garth shook her hand as he said his name. She had a strong grip and her hands were ice cold. "Oh, your hands are so warm," she said, "I am freezing in here. Where is your jersey? Are you not a Flames fan?" Garth said, "I will cheer for them but I am a Bruins fan at heart. I feel that if I wear another team's jersey that would be like cheating on a girlfriend."

Michelle giggled. "I admire that. I tend to cheer more for certain players than any one team." Garth looked at her jersey. "Who is number 7 for the Sharks?" he asked. Michelle turned her back to show the name. "Brad Stuart," she said. Garth frowned. He knew a lot of the players but he did not recognize this name. "He is from my hometown and my oldest sister used to baby sit him," she said. "Where is that?" he asked.

"Rocky Mountain House," she said, "do you know where that is?" Garth nodded. "Vaguely," he said, "I know it is west of Red Deer but I have never been there. I have heard it is a nice place, though."

"It is," she said, "you will have to make it a point to visit." "I will. But only if you will show me around," he said. Garth couldn't believe he said that. Michelle smiled and tilted her head. "Where are you from?" she said. "I am from a small town about an hour and a half southeast of Regina." "A flatlander," she said, "believe it or not, I have never been to Saskatchewan. So how about if you show me your town, I will show you mine." Michelle flashed her eyes. Garth looked into her brown eyes and returned the smile. "It's a deal," he said.

Ken wrapped his arm around Garth. "Hi Michelle, good to see you," said Ken, "I see you have met my little brother from another mother." "Yes, he has promised me to show me around his hometown," she said. "Well as long as that is the only thing he has promised to show you," said Ken, "come on Romeo let's get a beer. The Flames are out for their warm up."

Garth followed Ken into the luxury suite. The suite was long and narrow. At one end was a row of stools overlooking a half wall. Beyond the wall were 8 seats that looked out onto the ice. The room also sported a bar with tv and best of all the room had its own bathroom.

The night flew by for Garth. Most of the game he found himself sitting with Michelle. She took up most of his attention and before he wanted the game to end it was over. The rest of the group was headed to the Sorrel Horse for drinks after the game. "I would love to go but I have to be headed home," said Michelle, "I need to be up early for work tomorrow." Before Garth could say anything. Michelle handed him one of her business cards. "Give me a call. Maybe we can catch a movie or dinner," she said. "How about both," said Garth. Michelle smiled and squeezed his hand as she turned to leave.

Garth noticed her hands weren't cold anymore. "Geez Gibbers I didn't know you had it in you," said Ken, "come on let's go. The night is but a pup."

Chapter 4

Over the next couple of days, Garth worked hard on his pre-sentation. He reviewed the data he had before and was going through the process of gathering more data. He half-heartedly used the decline analysis that Big Dave wanted but not until he had figured out the curves from his own modelling program.

Garth's door was open, and he could see into the hallway outside his office. There were two men changing the pictures hanging on the walls. It was common for companies down-town to lease art for the office. Garth watched as they took down the picture that was outside of his office of a mango and a mouse pad. Garth had always considered it an eyesore and would be glad to see it go.

When Garth saw the painting they were putting up, he was surprised. It was a picture of a cherry blossom tree with an owl sitting on one of the branches. It was painted with vibrant colours and excellent detail. Garth wondered about the sym-bolism of this picture; the cherry blossom in Japan represented the fragility of life, and in some cultures, especially Native North American tribes, the owl represented death. Garth pon-dered for a moment, and he thought of the phrase from one of his favourite movies *The Shawshank Redemption* where Andy says to Red, "I guess it comes down to a simple choice: Get busy living or get busy dying."

A knock came at his door, and Garth looked up. He saw a tall, slender man with greying hair and large black-framed glasses standing in the doorway. Garth recognized who it was immediately; it was Terry Cooper, the Chief Reservoir Engineer at Maldere. "Hi Garth. You have a moment?" said Terry.

"Of course, come in, please," said Garth. Terry slid into his office, and the way he moved reminded Garth of a wraith.

"I see that you have a presentation coming up next week. I have been asked by Roger Maldere to go over it with you. Dave has had discussions with him saying that you were finding that the wells are at the optimum spacing already. I was wondering if you could walk me through your analysis and maybe I can provide some suggestions."

Garth felt the old pit in his stomach return, and he started to sweat. Terry said, "You see, Mr. Maldere has been presenting to shareholders at various conferences. He has been saying that we are going to be able to triple production out of these shallow gas areas with drilling over two thousand wells in the coming years. Obviously, this is a huge part of the plan to increase shareholder value along with the stock price. If we come out saying that this is not possible, we will get massacred on the stock exchange. This is something we want to avoid as nobody will benefit from that scenario."

Well, Garth thought, *at least I know what I am up against.* Garth pulled a chair around by his own chair so they could both view the computer screen. "Let me show you what I've got," said Garth.

Garth proceeded to go over the data and analysis that he had generated so far. Garth showed him the model he had created and how he was able to match the historical production to give him the estimates of original gas in place and remaining recoverable gas. Garth also showed the pressure information that he had received from Darcy. The pressures were declining at a significant rate at the current well spacing. The addition of more wells would lead to over capitalization and increase the rate of decline and acceleration of the reservoir depletion.

Garth was impressed with Terry as he intently listened and occasionally asked questions. Garth could tell that Terry understood what he was showing him. After about an hour, Terry leaned back in his chair and exclaimed, "Wow, this is pretty obvious."

"Garth, we are going to have to tread lightly with this one; let me see how we can proceed with this," said Terry. "The management is not going to like it."

"Why not?" asked Garth. "I can show that we can still add value with booster compression, reducing pressure drops, and by unloading water out of the wells. We don't have to drill many wells to do this."

"Garth, unfortunately the market doesn't care about that. The market wants to see that we have years of drilling locations. This shows to them that we have the ability to increase production over the coming years. Also, do you realize that the jobs of more than 50% of the people that work here depend on the drilling of wells? If we're not drilling wells, there is nothing for them to do," said Terry.

"What do you mean? Nobody cares about making money?" asked Garth.

"Let me put it to you this way: Drilling is like sex for most people, and you would be getting in the way of people having sex," said Terry.

"Tell you what I am going to do," said Terry. "I am going to get some third-party reserve evaluators in here to see what they come up with. That will take a couple of weeks so we will put the meeting off until then. The meeting will also include more people now from senior management."

"What do I tell Dave?" asked Garth.

"Let me worry about him," said Terry. "Let's stay in touch and keep working on this presentation together. Don't worry. We will get something figured out."

Terry rose from his chair and carried it back to its place in front of the desk. "Thanks, Garth," said Terry. "You have done some great work here. Unfortunately, it is not what people want to hear right now, so we've got to be prepared for that. We are going to get a lot of flak here and we need to get our ducks in a row."

Garth watched him leave. *Great. I do good work and nobody wants to hear it*, he thought. His gaze then turned to the painting in the hall. He concentrated on the owl and then let out a sigh and turned back to his computer.

The phone ringing startled Garth. He glanced at the number on the phone display and saw by the 306 area code that it was a Saskatchewan number that he did not recognize. He picked up the phone and said, "Hello, Garth Gibbins speaking."

The caller on the other end replied, "Garth, it's Uncle Dean. Don't freak out. I am calling from the Regina General Hospital. Your dad was brought here this morning. He had a heart attack. He is stable right now, but they are going to do a double bypass on him."

Garth felt the blood leaving his face and a pit in his stomach. "Oh my God," said Garth.

"I was with him when it happened," said Dean. "We were loading a grain truck. I walked around the tractor and saw him lying there. He was still conscious, and I raced him into Weyburn. They then took him by ambulance to Regina. He hasn't said much, other than he has been asking for you."

"Wow. Okay, Uncle. Tell Dad I love him, and I will be there as soon as I can," said Garth.

"Will do. See you Garth and drive safe. We'll be here," said Dean.

Garth hung up the phone with his trembling hand. He quickly gathered up the papers on his desk and organized them into binders. He glanced at the computer screen with his unfinished presentation. "It is just going to have to wait," Garth said to himself. He rushed out into the hall and looked towards Dave's office. Dave's door was open and Garth could see him sitting there.

Garth knocked and Dave looked up. "Come in Garth," said Dave. Dave had a quizzical look on his face as Garth stepped up to his desk.

"I just received a call from my uncle. My dad suffered a heart attack, and they have rushed him to the hospital. I am going to have to take some time off to be with him for a bit."

Dave studied Garth for a moment before he replied, "I am sorry to hear that. There is never a good time for something like that to happen. Hopefully he makes a speedy recovery. We have that presentation coming up in a week or so, you know. Just to be safe. Can you put what you have on the shared drive so we have access to it if you are not back in time," said Dave.

Garth hesitated for a moment before replying, "Sure, I can do that."

"Great," said Dave. "Also, can you check with HR before you leave and get everything straightened out with the time off?"

Garth nodded his head. "Thanks," said Garth, and he headed back out the door.

What an ass, thought Garth. But he guessed he shouldn't expect anything better from the likes of Dave. Garth went back to his office. He didn't move everything to the shared drive. Just enough of what he thought would satisfy Dave. The hell if Garth was going to give him access to everything.

Garth then thought, *Shit.* He just remembered he had bought tickets to take Michelle to the Tragically Hip this weekend. They had gone out on several dates since the Flames game, and Garth had planned a special evening for the two of them. He dialled her number and hoped she would answer as he did not want to have to leave a message.

On the third ring, he heard her voice say, "Hello, Michelle Newfield speaking."

"Hey Michelle, it's Garth."

"Hi Garth. Don't tell me you are calling to back out on me this weekend?" said Michelle.

Garth sighed and said, "Well actually, my dad has had a heart attack and is in the hospital in Regina. I am headed there right away. I'm sorry. You can have the Hip tickets and take a friend. I will call you when I get back. I am not sure when that will be – a week or so maybe."

Michelle said, "I am so sorry to hear that, Garth. I hope everything works out. Are you driving out there by yourself?"

"Thank you, Michelle," said Garth. "Yeah, I am driving by myself."

Michelle replied, "Okay, I will come over to your building and pick up the tickets. Again, I am so sorry. I will see you in front of your building in an hour."

Garth looked down at his watch. "Perfect, see you then," he said.

By the time Garth finished up with HR, close to an hour had elapsed. When he got to the bottom of the building, Michelle was waiting there for him. With a smile, she said, "I was asking my co-workers who wanted to go to the Hip. Crystal said she couldn't because she was going to see her folks in Regina this weekend. When I told her the situation, she said I could stay at her parents and come back with her on Sunday. So, how would you like some company for the trip? Tomorrow is our Golden Friday at work, and I have it off. Remember, you said you would take me to your hometown."

Garth was surprised. This was totally unexpected. He paused for a moment, and then he thought that the seven-and-a-half-hour drive was way better with some company – and good-looking company at that.

"Well, all right, but it won't be under the greatest of circumstances," said Garth.

"That's fine," replied Michelle. "I will be ready to go by three, and you can pick me up at my place." This picked up Garth's spirits immensely. Michelle hugged him tightly and said, "See you soon."

When he got home, he quickly threw what he thought would be enough clothes to last him two weeks into a suitcase. After thirty minutes, Garth pulled up to her house. It was a bungalow in an older neighbourhood with large spruce trees out front. He climbed up the concrete steps and rang the doorbell. Immediately, he could hear a dog start barking.

Within a couple of moments, he heard footsteps coming to the door. "Quiet Omar!" said Michelle and then the door opened. She had her long hair tucked up under a Toronto Blue Jays hat, and she wore faded jeans with a black shirt. Garth had never known how such a simple ensemble could look so amazing on a woman. When she looked up at his face, Garth took notice of her thick dark eyebrows that were displayed over her hazel eyes.

"Hi Garth. Sorry, this is my roommate's wiener dog, and he likes to bark when people ring the doorbell. If you don't mind, here is my suitcase. I will put him in his kennel, and I will be right out," said Michelle.

"No problem," said Garth, and he picked up the suitcase and carried it to the truck. He thought, *Holy crap, this thing is heavy.* No sooner had he placed the suitcase in the truck, when he looked back to see Michelle making her way down the sidewalk. Garth opened the truck door, and she climbed inside.

"Do you mind if I play some of my music?" Michelle asked.

"No, not at all," said Garth. Garth was surprised when she placed the CD into the player, and he heard the opening drums of "Run Runaway" by Slade.

"Oh my God," said Garth, "I love that song."

Michelle smiled and said, "Good. I have plenty more of that. Slade is my favourite band."

Garth said, "That's awesome. I always thought they were an under-rated band and should have got more recognition here. Quiet Riot's fame came from covering Slade songs."

Michelle said, "Yeah, I have always liked music that was a little bit out of the mainstream."

They had been driving and talking for about an hour when Michelle said, "Tell me more about your dad."

Garth's eyes went misty, as being with Michelle had taken his mind off his dad's situation. "Well, I guess we have a normal father and son relationship, where the son starts out thinking his dad is the greatest and wants to be just like him. Then the son gets into high school and thinks his dad knows nothing. After the son starts living in the real world, he notices how much smarter his dad has become," said Garth.

Michelle looked over at him and smiled. "In other words, the son thinks the dad has changed and grown when it is the son who changed."

Garth nodded. "Yeah. Those are the words. You know, when I was in high school, there were times I resented him. Blamed him for my mom leaving. It was tough. Looking back now, I realize how hard it was on him too."

"Why did your mom leave?" asked Michelle. Garth blinked and tears streamed down his cheeks. He quickly brushed them away. Michelle reached over and held his hand and said, "I am sorry if that is too personal, right now."

Garth managed a grin and said, "It's fine. I have never been able to talk like this with anyone before."

Garth let out a sigh and continued, "She got involved with another man. He never liked me much, and to be honest, the feeling was mutual. I know she never liked the farm, and maybe she knew I would never be happy in the city or with him around. She was probably right about that." Garth concentrated on the road, thinking hard. "You know, the ironic thing is that she was right," he said. "I loved the farm and wanted to stay there. Dad, on the other hand, didn't want me to have much to do with the farm and pushed me into Engineering. He is a farmer, but his dream was to be an engineer. I think he wanted us to have the same dream."

Garth looked out the window, as they drove through the rolling hills of the prairie west of Medicine Hat. In the hope of changing the subject, he pointed out some gas wells on the horizon. "You see there. Those are some of the gas wells I look after. The main compressor station is just over the hill," he said. "I wanted to install a booster compressor there to help push the gas over the hill, but my boss shot that idea down."

Michelle followed his gaze. "You know for someone who didn't want to be an engineer, you seem to be passionate about your work," said Michelle.

Garth smiled and replied, "I guess it is like they say: Sometimes you don't choose the career, the career chooses you."

"Hey, I want to show you a little tidbit of history," said Garth. He pulled the truck off the highway into a turn out. The sign that hung there was in a fading yellowish colour designed to look like parchment, complete with burnt edges. The sign read: "First Discovery of Natural Gas". Underneath the heading was a description of how gas had been mistakenly discovered there when the CPR was drilling for water for use in its locomotives.

Garth let Michelle read through the words written on the sign. When she finished, Garth asked, "See anything out of place on the sign?"

Michelle looked at him with a quizzical look then turned back to the sign. She re-read the sign and said, "Is the date of 1883 wrong? I thought the transcontinental railroad was finished in 1885?"

"I believe the date is correct," said Garth. "Do you notice anything suspicious about the depth at which they say they encountered the flow of natural gas?"

Michelle said, "3,250 metres?"

Garth nodded and said, "Yeah, just over three kilometres. That is quite a feat with a cable tool rig that they would have used in the 1800s. That is even a deep well for today's standards with a rotary rig," said Garth.

"What is it supposed to be then? 3,250 feet?" asked Michelle.

"It should read 325 metres. Somebody put the decimal in the wrong spot. I was told it was because the sign was put up in the 70s," said Garth.

Michelle smiled and said, "Oh, because the guy that made it was high?"

Garth laughed, "Well, maybe. It was right at the time we converted from the Imperial system to the metric system, and apparently, somebody screwed up the conversion from feet to metres."

Now it was Michelle's turn to laugh. "Probably an engineer did the conversion. Didn't NASA lose a Mars Orbiter recently because someone used the wrong units?"

"Yeah, they did. Even the smartest people miss the small stuff from time to time," said Garth.

The sun was setting and darkness was encroaching. Michelle said, "Is there a bathroom around here?"

Garth gestured with his hands and said, "Thousands."

Michelle smiled, "Seriously?"

Garth shook his head and said, "I am sorry, my lady, but we are still forty-five minutes from Medicine Hat, and there ain't much else until we get there. Here, take some tissue. I will keep watch here." Michelle opened the door. "Watch the cactus," said Garth. Michelle just gave a nervous laugh and disappeared on the other side of the sign.

She got back to the truck and said, "Well, I see this is a popular stop for people from Saskatchewan."

It was Garth's turn to be quizzical. "What do you mean?" he asked.

"There are a couple of Pilsner bottles smashed back there. Isn't that Saskatchewan champagne?" she asked.

Garth laughed, "You know, I never heard that until I moved to Alberta. The only people I ever knew who drank Pilsner were from Medicine Hat." They continued back onto the highway. "I guess being secluded in Saskabush, I never realized how much others made fun of people from Saskatchewan. You know bunny hugs, grid roads, sloughs, Pilsner, Riders, and the like. Well, except the Riders part is quite true; that is like a religion."

When they drove past a deer crossing sign, it brought to Garth's mind something from another province that was odd to him but that nobody seemed to care about. "Do you see that sign?" said Garth. Michelle nodded. "What type of deer is that supposed to be?" asked Garth.

Michelle shrugged, "I am not really sure. Should be an antelope sign out here," she said.

"That sign shows a deer, but I don't even know what it is. My best guess is that it is a red deer, which is not native to North America and has no business being on a deer crossing sign here. In Alberta, you will see lots like these. I have even seen some that more closely resemble a reindeer. In Saskatchewan, the deer crossing signs can easily be recognized as a white-tailed deer," said Garth.

Michelle just looked at him and flashed a hint of a smirk and said, "So I am guessing you are not a fan of the *Deer Hunter* movie?"

Garth couldn't help but laugh out loud. "Wow I can't believe you know that one," he said.

Michelle continued, "My dad is a hunter, and it drove him nuts how they were hunting deer in what was supposed to be Pennsylvania, and the deer were red deer. He could never get over the fact that it won Best Picture. He took pride in the fact that the next movie that guy directed bombed."

Garth said, "I think I will like your dad."

"I have been thinking. Everything we just talked about – the deer signs, *Deer Hunter*, music – it all boils down to one simple thing about human nature," said Garth.

Michelle laughed. "What are you talking about?"

Garth looked over at her and smiled, "People will follow along with anything, as they do not want to be seen as not fitting in or stupid with what society considers to be acceptable."

Michelle leaned over and grabbed a hold of Garth's hand as they drove. She said, "Kind of like the 'Emperor's New Clothes'."

Garth grinned, "Yes exactly." Garth chuckled to himself about how this old tale seemed to fit in with so much of his life.

It was getting quite dark now as they got closer to Regina. They could see the lights from a distance. Normally it felt like it was taking forever to make the last couple of miles, but not tonight. Garth didn't want the drive to end.

Garth made the turn from the ring road on to Albert Street towards the hotel where his Uncle Dean was staying. They were both starved because, aside from snacks they had picked up along the way when they stopped for fuel, they had not eaten anything. There was a lounge on the main floor they had noticed when they came in through the lobby. They decided to head there for a much needed drink and a bite to eat. Garth phoned Dean's room, but there was no answer, so he left a message telling him where they would be.

The lounge was not busy, aside from a couple at one of the tables and two businessmen sitting at the bar. Garth and

Michelle took a seat at a table for four. The waitress came over to take their drink order and handed out menus. The waitress turned to get their drinks and Garth saw his Uncle Dean walk into the room.

"Jimmy, how the hell are you? And who is this warm cup of sunshine? I didn't think they made hitchhikers this beautiful anymore," said Dean.

Garth rose from his chair and shook his Uncle Dean's hand. "Uncle Dean, I would like you to meet Michelle," said Garth.

"Pleasure to meet you, Michelle," said Dean as he extended his big meaty hand.

"Same here," said Michelle. She looked over at Garth and gave a quizzical look. "Jimmy?" she said. "Is that your middle name?"

Dean let go a hearty laugh and said, "No darling. That is a nickname I gave him a long time ago. He could never leave any toy alone. He had to 'jimmy' with it to figure out how it worked. Never satisfied, I guess."

Michelle laughed. "You are telling me that he was an engineer from a young age and didn't even know it."

Dean nodded. "You got it," he said. "Garth, you better be careful. This young lady is probably out of your league."

"How is Dad doing?" asked Garth.

"Well he is doing as well as you could hope for, I guess. They put a stent in the main artery this afternoon. I can't remember which one the doctor said. The doctor seems to be happy with how everything went. He expects your dad to make a full recovery, but he will have to lay low for six to eight weeks. Hopefully they will release him from the hospital on Monday," said Dean.

"Your dad is in good spirits though, and I know he will be really glad to see you," said Dean.

"Has Christine been there to see him?" asked Garth.

"No. Your mom is on vacation in California right now apparently," said Dean. "She does know. You haven't talked to her?"

Garth shook his head. "I haven't talked to her for a couple of months. She usually calls me when she starts to feel sorry for herself." Garth could feel Michelle's eyes watching him as he held back tears.

"I had better phone Crystal," said Michelle, "and let her know I am in town." She got up and made her way to the lobby phone.

"Great girl," said Dean. "Your dad will think so too."

Garth said, "Thanks, Uncle. Yes. She is."

Dean continued. "See moving to Calgary wasn't a total loss." They were both laughing when Michelle returned.

"All good to go," said Michelle. "Mr. Gibbins, it was a pleasure to meet you."

Dean rose and gave her a hug. "My dad is Mr. Gibbins. Please call me Dean," he said. "And believe me, the pleasure is all mine to make your acquaintance, Michelle." Dean then turned to Garth and said, "I will meet you in the lobby at say eight. Then we can pick this pretty lady up and head out for breaky."

"Sounds good," said Garth. "Good night, Uncle."

Garth and Michelle made their way to Garth's truck. "Your uncle is a nice and funny man. I can see that you really look up to him, don't you?" said Michelle.

"I sure do. I don't know how my life would have been if Uncle Dean hadn't been there for me. He was the glue that kept everything together."

The next morning after picking up Michelle, the three of them went for breakfast in a restaurant close to the hospital. The hospital was located on the southeast side of the downtown core area. It had been constructed on this site in the early 1900's and still enjoyed a historic look to it. It was a sprawling, red brick building complex with six floors that covered an area of about four and a half city blocks.

After being unable to find a parking space on the street next to the hospital, Dean squeezed his Dodge truck into a parking spot between an old Ford Tempo and a Ford Ranger pickup in the hospital parking lot. "Well, here we are," said Dean as he masterfully parallel parked. When they were making their way to the main entrance, Dean stopped and looked back at his Dodge truck sandwiched in between the two Fords. "Well, look at that. A rose between two thorns," he said. Garth just shook his head and laughed. That was what he loved most about his uncle – his endless sense of humour.

They walked through the sliding doors and past the admitting desk. Garth cringed as the hospital smell of the disinfectant and cleaners they used hit his nostrils. As usual, the smell was nauseating and offensive.

They made their way to the elevator and up to the third floor. They walked down the corridor and entered one of the rooms. There, lying on a bed against the wall, was Jack Gibbins. He was dressed in a white with purple flecks hospital gown. His hair was matted, and his skin was as white as a ghost. Garth thought if he got up and walked around at night, someone would surely mistake him for one of the ghosts that were said to haunt the hospital.

Jack looked at them with sunken eyes and managed a wry smile. He looked at Michelle and said, "Why hello there, gorgeous. You must be lost or I am dead because you look like an angel. But I am leaning to lost, because if you are an angel, that would mean we are all in heaven, and I know that ain't happening with this crew."

Michelle gave the slightest of a blush and looked down momentarily. She responded by saying, "Well, I can see the elder Gibbins men are quite the charmers. Not sure what happened to this one," as she nodded her head towards Garth.

They all laughed at the expression on Garth's face. Garth, however, now felt as big as a grain of wheat. "Go easy on him. I hear it skips a generation. At least we know he has great taste," said Jack.

Michelle smiled and grasped Garth's hand and gave it a squeeze. Garth felt a wave of warm delight flow through his body as he felt her hand in his.

Garth walked around to the right side of the hospital bed. Jack grabbed his free hand and gave a feeble clasp. Garth returned the gesture and thought to himself that this was only the second time he could remember shaking hands with his dad. The other time had been when he graduated from high school, and the graduates had gone into the crowd to thank their parents as part of the ceremony.

They talked about Jack's condition and how he was coping. Finally, after about an hour, Dean said, "Why don't I take Michelle downstairs for a coffee and doughnut and we can leave you two alone for a while."

This puzzled Garth for a moment, but Michelle quickly said, "That sounds good. Do you want us to bring you guys back anything?"

"I will have a coffee," said Garth.

"And I will take a maple-dip doughnut," smiled Jack.

"I think you should probably pass on the doughnut, bro, considering you are in here for a doughnut plug in the plumbing already," smiled Dean. They all laughed at this.

Jack replied, "I suppose you are right. But now that they fixed the plumbing, I should be good to go again."

Michelle got up and left with Dean. Garth watched them as they walked out of the room. He looked back at his dad, who was being jovial this morning. Garth wondered if it was the painkillers he was on, as he hadn't seen him this upbeat in a long time.

Garth took a seat in the visitor chair nearest his dad's bed. His dad feebly grabbed his hand and said, "Garth, I know I have been hard on you growing up. I want you to know that I love you, and I am very proud of you." Garth could feel tears beginning to form in his eyes. He had waited years to hear those words. His dad continued, "I know you feel as if I pushed you into Engineering, but I only wanted you to be the best you could. I always felt you were capable of doing more with your life than I did." Garth blinked and looked at his dad. Through the years, a small part of him had resented his dad for forcing him into Engineering when really all he ever wanted to do was farm.

"I saw something in you and knew you would be a good engineer, and I was right," said Jack.

"I always tried to do what you asked of me, Dad, but I still think I could have been a good farmer," said Garth. Jack smiled and said, "I know you would have been good at that too. But you must have felt something deep down as well, because you could have said, 'No, I am not going to take Engineering.'" This comment struck Garth. He had never thought it that simple. All this time he had been blaming his dad, when in reality the choice had been ultimately his.

Just as Garth was about to reply, a tall blonde-haired nurse entered the room. Garth guessed she was in her early thirties. "Hello, Mr. Gibbins. How are you feeling? How is your pain level on a scale of 1-10?" said the nurse.

"I feel fine. My pain is about a 4, I would say," replied Jack.

"Good. We will keep your pain meds at the same level. Now I am going to check your blood pressure again." As the nurse moved around the bed to apply the cuff to Jack's arm, she said, "And who is this young man?"

Jack looked back at Garth and said, "This here is my son, Garth. He just came here from Calgary."

"Hello, Garth. My name is Lana, and I am the charge nurse for this unit. You know your dad is a lucky man. He suffered what we call the widow maker."

"What is the widow maker?" asked Garth.

"It is when the left anterior descending artery or LAD becomes blocked, cutting off blood supply to the heart. Normally only one out of ten survives this heart attack, hence the name 'widow maker'," said Lana.

"Thankfully, there was no widow to be made as I am single," joked Jack. Lana gave a small chuckle and said, "Either way, you are very lucky." Lana finished up her check of Jack's vital signs and said she would be back when it was time for Jack to eat.

Garth was glad that the nurse had come in at that time as it gave him some time to think of a reply to his dad. "Thanks, Dad. It means a lot to me to hear what you said. I know you only wanted me to challenge myself and be the best I could be. But I am going to play farmer all next week and help Dean out as much as I can. And there is nothing you can say to stop me," said Garth.

"Okay, I concede. Thanks, Garth. It will be great to have you around," said Jack. This time it was Garth who reached out to squeeze Jack's hand, and in that moment, Garth felt that he had finally made peace with his dad and at the same time with himself as well.

Michelle and Dean came back to the room, and the four of them talked about many topics, but Garth thought the conversations leaned more towards telling embarrassing stories about Garth for Michelle. When Jack's food arrived, Michelle and Garth decided it was a good time for them to stretch their legs.

They headed to the main floor of the hospital, and Michelle said she needed to find a washroom. As Garth waited for her, he noticed a stand that had been set up next to the doughnut shop. The stand was for First Nations artifacts and was behind a sign that read, "Profits for Survivors of the Gordon Indian Residential School." Garth remembered that the Aboriginal residential schools were boarding schools where the First Nations children were sent in order to assimilate them into Canadian culture and away from their own heritage. The schools were detrimental to the children that went there, as the children were not only taken from their families but also abused in many cases, both physically and sexually. Thousands of children had died in attendance at these boarding houses. This particular school at Punnichy, on the alphabet railway, was one of the last ones to finally shut down.

As Garth looked over the many handmade artifacts, he couldn't help but notice that the old First Nations man behind the counter was staring at him. Finally, the man got up and walked over to Garth. He had long white hair, a large bulbous nose, and cheeks that were pockmarked and showed many scars. Garth looked up into the man's bloodshot eyes that seemed to pierce right through his soul. Garth felt a cold shiver run up his spine and he felt uncomfortable.

"I am sorry. I did not mean to scare you. I see that you are looking at this owl totem necklace," said the man. The black braided leather necklace had a pendant that had a totem carving that was a couple of inches long with the owl as the main animal. "I think the owl suits you well," he said. Garth was taken aback by this statement, as in most First Nations traditions the owl is the messenger of death.

"Isn't the owl a symbol of a bad omen," said Garth.

"The owl represents a change. To many, changes are bad," said the man, "but the owl also represents intuition. In that, one has the ability to see what others cannot and can see beyond masks and deceit. As I can see in your eyes, you are able to see what others do not or choose not to. Take this owl as a reminder of your ability, as I see that it is going to face a great challenge in the near future."

Garth was in awe as he listened to the old man talk and thought back to the painting that hung outside his office. Just then, he felt Michelle walk up behind him. She looked over his shoulder and said, "That is beautiful. You should buy that." The old man's face contorted into a wrinkled smile, and he nodded. Garth dug the twenty-five dollars out of his wallet and handed it the man. The man took it, shook his hand, and handed Garth the pendant. "God bless you, and thank you," the man said as he turned back to take his place on the stool.

"I phoned Crystal," said Michelle. "She had some friends over, and it sounded like they were having a party. Would it be alright if we stopped in and grabbed my stuff? I don't feel like staying there if they are going to be partying. I can get a room at the hotel."

Garth shrugged, "That's fine."

Later that night, after they had visited with Jack again, the three headed back to the hotel. It was after 9:00 p.m. when they arrived back at the hotel. Michelle went to the desk and got her own room. Dean gestured to the lounge and said, "Well, guys, how about a night cap?"

Michelle said, "I am feeling pretty tired. I think I will head on up to bed, but you two go on if you like."

Garth was about to head to the lounge when Dean stopped him. Michelle's back was to them as she waited for the elevator. Dean mouthed to Garth, "Go with her," and gave him a push in her direction.

Garth stammered, "I think I will head up with you as well."

Dean said, "Alright kids, have a good night," and he turned and walked into the lounge. Garth and Michelle both said good night to him. Before the elevator arrived, they could hear Dean say to the waitress, "Hello darling, I am feeling a little bit parched as it has been a long day. What do you have on tap?"

The elevator arrived, and they both got on. Michelle was shaking her head, "What a charmer your uncle is."

They arrived on Michelle's floor. As the elevator doors opened, Michelle leaned into him and delivered a deep, passionate kiss. "Why don't you come tuck me in," she said. She grabbed Garth by the hand and led him to her room. Garth's heart clamoured in his chest. He felt as if he was someone else as he followed her into the room.

Chapter 5

Garth spent the next week in his glory. He had seen Michelle off as she headed back to Calgary with Crystal. He went back to the farm with Dean and Jack. Garth never realized just how much he missed the smell of diesel, the sound of the meadowlark, and the sight of a bright orange sunrise with the morning chill. Jack had been released from the hospital, and Dean and Garth tried their best to make sure he rested. Jack and Garth's relationship changed overnight and became more like friends than just father and son.

Garth enjoyed the farm, but he missed Michelle terribly and longed to return to Calgary. Eventually he found himself back on the train headed towards the downtown. He was feeling pretty good about himself, and not even a packed train was going to deter him. Even when he got off the platform, he did not try to avoid the homeless man, and he handed him $5. The homeless man said, "Oh thank you, and God bless."

Garth moved along through the other commuters towards the Tim Hortons. He stepped through the door into the Tim's and took his place at the end of the line. "Gibbers!" came a call from behind him. Garth didn't need to turn around to know that Ken was coming in behind him.

"Kenny, what's shaking?" said Garth.

"First of all, how is your dad?" said Ken.

"He is doing pretty good now. I think this experience has really changed him for the better," said Garth.

"Good. Well, speaking of change. You are about to get a big change in your world," said Ken.

"What do you mean?" asked Garth.

"You probably haven't heard. We bought out Bear Creek Resources, and they have a bunch of gas in your area," said Ken.

"They were the ones that outbid us at the land sale last year. Big Dave was absolutely pissed, saying we had severely under-valued it," said Garth.

"Yep. Those are the guys. I guess they tested some good wells on it," said Ken.

Garth felt the bottom of his stomach fall out and started to feel lightheaded as he felt the blood flow leaving his head. "What did we pay for it?" asked Garth.

"Well, I believe Bear Creek paid about one thousand dollars per acre last year at the land sale, and from the numbers, it looks like we are paying twice that much for the company," said Ken.

"Jesus, I hope they have other stuff than that shallow gas," said Garth.

"They do. How I heard it though is we paid a premium to have those shallow gas assets," said Ken.

"Great," said Garth. "I am guessing there is hell to pay now for why we didn't buy it a year ago."

Ken nodded his head. "Yes. I am sure Big Dave will want to see you this morning."

Well, thought Garth, *there goes the good mood.*

Garth paid for their coffees and walked back to the office. Garth exited the elevator and headed to his office. He noticed that Big Dave was in his office, going through a bunch of files. "Garth," came the call from Big Dave.

"Yes, Dave," said Garth.

"I am glad you are back. A lot has happened since you were away. We bought Bear Creek Resources, and we are going to have a meeting this morning to go over the assets and what our plans for it are. I am going to need you to bring your analysis of the land sale we did last year where they outbid us. The upper management wants to see it," said Dave.

"Okay. Who did the engineering analysis for this acquisition?" asked Garth.

"Tyler Henderson was the Engineer. It was done at a high level, so only a few people knew about it. I didn't even know they were looking at it," said Dave. This day was just getting better by the moment for Garth. Of all the people that had to evaluate the acquisition, of course, it had to be that asshole Tyler. "The meeting is at 10:00 a.m. in the main boardroom. I will see you there," said Dave. Dave then turned back to his files he was pouring over.

Garth took this as the time to leave and went into his office. He sat down on his desk and looked back through the door. The first thing he saw was the owl painting. It reminded him of the owl pendant he had purchased in Regina. He leafed through his leather satchel and pulled out the pendant. He turned it over and over in his hand as he thought back to the old First Nations man he had bought it from. *Challenge ahead alright.* He hung the pendant over his computer monitor and opened up his file cabinet that contained his land sale backup files.

Garth spent the rest of the morning gathering up the work he had done on the land sale and work he had done since. He placed it all into a three-hole binder and looked at the time on his office phone display. It was 9:51 – time for him to head to the boardroom. He collected his things and headed out the door.

He had only been to the main boardroom once before, which just so happened to be for the land sale in question. The main boardroom was located on the 28th floor, which was the top floor where the top brass had their offices. The 28th floor was completely different from the rest of the floors. It had marble pillars and cathedral arches, and here the floors were white marble with plush carpet in the offices. These offices were four times the size of an office on the floors where the employees sat. It reminded Garth of something out of the Roman Empire. If it was meant to intimidate, it certainly was effective.

The first person that Garth saw was Terry Cooper. At least there was one friendly face in this crowd. "Hi Garth, how is your dad?" asked Terry.

"He is doing quite well, all things considered. Thanks for asking," said Garth.

"No rest for the wicked, eh? You get to be right back into it with this meeting," said Terry. Terry glanced down to the armful of papers and the binder that Garth was carrying. "Well at least you brought lots of ammo," said Terry.

"In God we trust. Everybody else bring data," said Garth. Garth saw some heads turn from the other people in the room. None of them seemed to be amused.

Terry chuckled and said, "Never be surprised by what people will believe in."

Terry and Garth took a seat at the boardroom table beside one another. Garth looked around the room at the others that were mingling about. Most of them were dressed in suit and ties. Garth felt under-dressed in his casual khakis and polo shirt. If he would have known beforehand about this meeting, he could have dressed himself in a tie at least. He saw some of the upper management there that he had never actually met, but he knew who they were. There was Ellen Sheard, who was the Vice President of Exploration. She was in her mid-forties, but the darkness under her eyes from years of lack of sleep suggested to the unknowing that she was much older. She carried a reputation for being ruthless in a meeting and for throwing people under the bus who dared to disagree with her. She was talking to Bill Yen, who was the COO for Maldere. He was older than Ellen, short, thin, and moved about like he was in great pain. Rumour was that he had a bad case of arthritis in his spine, making movement difficult and painful. People often joked his pain was caused from the years of Roger Maldere pulling his puppet strings.

Seated at the table was Tim Kane, who had a huge frame and to Garth looked more like a bodybuilder than the Vice President of Engineering. He was completely bald and sported a grey goatee. Garth heard when he used to play hockey they called him Ulf. This was in reference to Ulf Samuelson, who was known as a dirty player. Others at Maldere called him Mr. Clean, as nothing ever stuck to him, and he had a reputation of cleaning house when things did not go his way. One story that often was told about Tim was that in a meeting at one of the field offices, some of the employees had requested a meeting with him. They then proceeded to tell him some of their grievances and ideas on how to make things better. After the meeting, Tim had thanked them for their input and said how his door is always open to meet with anyone. Then he walked down the hallway to the foreman's office and told him to fire every one of them, which the foreman reluctantly did. No one requested a one-on-one meeting with him again.

Next to Tim Kane, was Dave Shaw the Business Development Manager. Garth assumed he was the one who had negotiated the deal with Bear Creek. Dave Shaw had a thick head of greying hair that was expertly groomed and slicked down with enough gel to survive a wind tunnel test. To Garth he looked like a big goof. Tim and Dave were talking, and every now and then, one of them would look at Garth. Garth knew they were talking about him.

Garth took out his binder and opened it to his analysis of the land sale and started rummaging through the pages to try and relax himself. He was extremely nervous about what was going to transpire. Then he caught movement at the door and saw Dave Piett and Tyler Henderson laughing and joking as they made their way into the boardroom. Dave Piett took a seat right next to Garth.

Garth looked down at his watch, and it was now 10:02. Roger Maldere strode into the room, and everyone looked his way and took a seat. It was as if the Emperor himself had blessed everyone with his appearance. Maldere said, "Let's get this show on the road. I have to do a teleconference call at 12:00. Dave, please get us started." Dave Shaw stood up and turned on the projector and started his presentation.

Dave Shaw walked them through a summary of the acquisition, particularly focusing on the shallow gas area to the southwest of what Maldere already owned. Dave Shaw called it a tucked-in acquisition that tied together with what they already owned. They had identified over two thousand drilling locations, giving them over five years of drilling inventory. Garth looked around the room and saw everyone was nodding their head in approval – everyone that was except for him and Terry. In fact, he thought Terry's face was turning redder than the red tie he had on.

Dave finished and said, "Now I will turn this over to Tyler Henderson to go over the engineering details of why this is such a good acquisition for Maldere." Tyler stood up and took the laser pointer from Dave's hand.

"Thank you, Dave," said Tyler. "Bear Creek did an excellent job of evaluating this unconventional play that we missed out on last year." Tyler looked right at Garth as he said it. Garth just glared back at him. "I say unconventional in that conventional engineering techniques do not apply. The gas is trapped within the shale, which has low permeability, microdarcies in fact. From my experience in working tight gas plays in Texas, I found that the shallow gas in this region is similar and calls for the same exploitation – that being tight down-spacing and large sand fracs. From our analysis, the shallow gas in this area has about ten Bcf of reserves in place per section and that it will be necessary to drill up to thirty-two wells per section to recover this large gas in place. These shallow gas reserves are like a gas farm, as when the pressure is dropped in the shale reservoir, it will expel more gas from the shale and regenerate reserves."

Garth fidgeted in his seat. *Are these people believing this*? He looked around the room again and saw that the answer was yes. They were eating it up like pumpkin pie at a Thanksgiving dinner.

Tyler continued. "Bear Creek drilled and tested twelve wells here to the southwest of our lands, and those twelve wells tested anywhere from one hundred and twenty-five Mcf per day to three hundred and fifty Mcf per day on twenty-four hour flow tests. With these rates and reserves and a gas forecast going to seven dollars per Mcf, these wells will pay out in ten months."

At this Ellen interjected, "Why are these rates better than what we have on our lands. Shouldn't our lands be better?"

Tyler answered, "Yes, they should be. If we apply the Bear Creek knowledge to our own lands, I believe we will see better results than what we have been doing."

Tim said, "So what are they doing different?"

"They are opening up more zone in the Milk River and Medicine Hat formations and hitting them with four times the tonnage of sand than what we are currently doing. We seem to have focused more on the Second White Specks in this area for some reason and are missing a big piece of the pie."

As Tyler said this last statement, everyone turned to look at Garth. Roger Maldere was the first to speak and said, "Terry why have we not been doing this?"

Terry said, "Well, I think it is best that Garth go through his analysis to show you what we think is going on."

Garth cleared his throat and began to speak. He knew he sounded nervous, but he managed to say, "We have focused on the Second White Specks as the Milk River and Medicine Hat formations tend to be wet as you head in a southwest direction off of our lands. The Second White Specks tends to get wetter as well, but we have found there are some offshore marine bars that have been preserved that produce gas, but they are linear trends. They are not wide, and if you get off of them, you are back into water."

Ellen was the first to cut him off, "How can you say that it gets wetter as you go to the Southwest? It gets shallower as you move that way, and if I understand gravity correctly, which I think I do, gas sits on top of water. What you are saying makes no sense."

Garth said, "Well Tyler is right in that this play is unconventional, but not for the reasons that he has said. The trapping mechanism here is what is called a 'deep basin trap'. It is true that the formations get shallower as you move to the southwest. They also generally get better permeability to where they outcrop, for example, the Milk River outcrops in the south. The rock carvings and paintings at Writing on Stone are made on the Milk River sandstone outcrops. The Milk River formation is the water aquifer that farmers get their water from north of there.

"In some places, there is some gas in it as some farmers have been known to be able to light the gas from their water wells. The pioneers used to joke that it was so dry that even the water burns. Water moves as far as the permeability can support it, so generally, the more permeable the rock, the more water it produces. The tighter the rock is, the more gas and less water there is. As you go to the northeast, there is more gas, but the rock becomes less permeable, so the deliverability is lower. What you want for a productive reservoir is not too good, as it will be wet but not too bad or it won't produce anything."

As Garth said this, he could see he was losing the audience by their glazed-over expressions.

"So you are telling me that we need to be looking for Goldilocks of the shallow gas reservoirs," sneered Roger Maldere. Everyone laughed at this and looked back at Garth with amused but disinterested faces. "I have worked shallow gas for more than thirty years. I know there is no water in these formations, except for maybe water of condensation."

Garth interjected, "Well, we tested wells in this area that we had just bought, and they produced a barrel per hour of water with little to no gas from the Milk River. That's a lot of water by condensation." As Garth said it, he knew he had crossed the line.

"Young man, I believe those wells were not completed with the right fluid system, and what you were getting back was completion fluid or they were fracked out of zone into another formation. Besides, at the time they were completed, the consultant was a fellow by the name of "Zip" Jarvis. We called him "Zip" because he zipped through the completions without adequately testing the wells before condemning them," snapped back Roger Maldere. "I think you need to go back and look over your wells. I suggest you get Tyler here to help you. I want to see a development plan where we apply the Bear Creek system on our own lands, as I believe we probably have over ten thousand locations on our own land. What are we estimating for gas reserves on our land?" said Roger.

"About five and a half Bcf per section," replied Garth.

"If the Bear Creek lands have over ten Bcf per section, our lands should have at least that. I am guessing more," said Roger. "Would you say our lands probably have the potential to be greater than ten Bcf per section?"

Garth thought for a moment, and then he felt like somebody else spoke when he said, "Well, if you ignore the production data, pressure information, core evaluations, well logs, and drill stem tests. I suppose."

Instead of getting mad, Roger simply replied, "Good, so even you are saying there is a chance." Garth couldn't believe his ears.

Then Roger said to everyone in the boardroom, "Great acquisition, everyone. I want a presentation put together that details the drilling potential on the lands we are acquiring but also what potential we have on our lands. I think we should be able to double our production corporately in five years, and that is what I am going to tell the analysts in the teleconference." Everyone except Terry and Garth nodded their heads in approval.

Roger Maldere then got up and left the room. As he left, Ellen turned to Garth and said, "Garth, I think you should spend more time on how you are going to increase shareholder value. Your method of slow and methodical is not what we need. We need to be showing growth, and you really need to believe in the properties."

Garth said, "I do believe in the properties, but since I turned eight, I don't believe in fairy tales."

Nobody laughed at this and Ellen replied, "I think you need to realize that we are trying to help you, and if you don't fall in line, you are going to find yourself standing outside wanting back in." With that, the room cleared one by one. As Tyler walked by he said, "Hey Gibbins, whenever you want to learn how to do real engineering, book a time with me."

That son of a bitch, thought Garth.

Terry remained behind. He said, "Sorry, Garth. I didn't know it was going to be like that. When you are part of a public company, it seems to be more about creating the illusion of value than actually creating real value. Real value is what you create. But as they say, you sell the sizzle and not the steak.

That pretty much sums up the focus of a public company. Come on! Let's go get a beer somewhere."

They left the boardroom, and Terry told Garth to meet him on the ground floor outside of the elevators in ten minutes. Garth went back to his office. He made sure to go the long way so as not to have to walk past Big Dave's office. He could see that Dave was in his office with the door closed and was talking to someone. Through the muffled voices, Garth could hear through the wall that it was Tyler to whom Dave was talking. Garth dropped off his binder and papers and quickly got out of the office. He did not want to see or talk to anyone.

Garth managed to make it down the elevator without meeting anyone. Once there, Terry was already waiting for him. "How does the Einhorn pub sound?" asked Terry.

"Sure, sounds good," replied Garth. The Einhorn was about four blocks away, and they walked in silence most of the way. The Einhorn was located off 8th Avenue, which during the day only allowed pedestrian and cycle traffic. Many of the pubs along the way had patio seating, which gave an inviting and pleasant atmosphere to sip on suds in the sun and people watch. Today, however, they would be having their beverages in peace downstairs. Terry opened the large heavy wooden door and held it for Garth to go through. They walked down the stairs. Garth looked around, and there were only a couple of patrons seated at the bar. A waitress that was wrapping cutlery in napkins in preparation for the lunch crowd turned to them and said, "Take a seat anywhere."

Terry and Garth took a seat at a booth in the back. The pub was dimly lit, with a large oak bar that was set in a rectangle shape in the middle of the room. The walls were made of stone, and the ceiling was open with heavy wooden beams running throughout. The pub gave off a traditional, rustic, German ambiance.

The waitress came over and took their orders. When she brought the pints of beer back to the table, Terry said, "You know, Garth, I have worked for Maldere my whole career, which is going on over twenty years now. If I can give you advice, it is not to take anything too personal. I know that sounds hard to do, since we spend most of our waking hours at work, and our life revolves around it, but you have to remember this is a huge game to most of these guys, and you and I are just playing pieces that can either be sacrificed or managed for a positional advantage. Money to these guys is the trophy you get for playing the game. Of course, like any trophy it is a bragging right that they can flaunt around at the Petroleum Club, saying, "Look at me, I made this much money, so I am better than you. These guys are competitive, and when you are that competitive and focused on money, common sense gets replaced by gambler's intuition."

Garth didn't say a word as he listened intently, in between taking sips of beer. Terry continued, "Now Roger is a smart guy. He wouldn't be where he is, if he wasn't. But after people have had success, something within seems to change. A feeling of invincibility comes over them, and they constantly want their ego stroked. They forget what got them there and will surround themselves with people who will always affirm how great they are. It kind of is like the Emperor's new clothes, where no one will speak up for fear of being seen as incompetent or stupid and falling out of favour with the Emperor. If you remember the story of the "Emperor's New Clothes", you are the kid that yelled, "He's naked."

Garth continued to sip his beer as he thought of something his grandfather used to say. Garth asked, "It has been said there is a thin line between genius and stupidity; do you know what that line is?"

Terry looked at Garth and then took a long drink of his beer. He set the glass back on the table and said, "I believe it is that genius has limitations, right?"

Garth smiled and said, "Yes, that is the difference. The separating factor though, is money."

Terry laughed and said, "That is so true. People with money seem to lose their moral compass, as well as normal perception and the ability for social interaction." Terry continued, "Roger is a Geologist by trade. Geologists tend to be optimistic. I believe they kind of must be in order to have the ability to take the risky step of drilling wells. Roger formed Maldere when he was relatively young and was able to raise financing with the help of his father, who also had been successful in the oil patch. He had success right out of the gate when they bought some oil assets when the price of oil was low.

"Within a couple of months, the oil price doubled, which kick-started Maldere's transformation into a major player. Roger changed after that. A hard-core Geologist pouring over net pay maps and seismic lines was replaced with an attention-loving, self-centered CEO. He bought a large house on the Elbow River and a bunch of expensive cars and went through women like you wouldn't believe. It was so bad that at one Christmas party he did three women that worked for us."

"Yeah, I heard about that," said Garth.

"Anyways," continued Terry, "dealing with these types of guys is difficult. Unlike you and me, they don't think rationally. When they are presented with facts, they can quickly shoot holes in them, because they have already made up in their minds what the facts are. Their job is to be able to spin those 'facts' into some story that potential investors will believe. For example, companies when showing the perceived success of an oil program will only show the oil production and not the water production or gas production. They don't want to lift their dress over their head and show that the water cut is over 90% and climbing or that the gas/oil ratio is climbing out of sight. They really are magicians in tricking your mind into what they want you to see."

"It's like a house of cards, isn't it," said Garth.

"Exactly, the whole thing can collapse if even one card is shifted out of place," said Terry. "My suggestion is to go ahead and meet with Tyler, no matter how much you don't want to, and find out everything you can about their analysis technique and procedures. You may find something you can use that will help you in the argument. As Sun Tzu said in his book *The Art of War*, one of the keys to winning a battle is to know your enemy as well as you know yourself," said Terry.

Garth thought a moment. He had heard of the book *The Art of War* but had never read it. Maybe it was time he read it. "I would rather punch old Tyler in the face, set him on fire, and piss on his ashes," said Garth.

"Why don't you tell me how you really feel?" laughed Terry. "That might make you feel better for the moment, but I think it would be more satisfying to beat them at their own game."

Garth and Terry stayed all afternoon at the pub and never went back to work. After 5:00 p.m., they finally left as Terry said he needed to get home for his daughter's soccer game that night. Garth walked to the train station and rode it to the closest stop to Michelle's place. Garth had phoned her in advance, and she met him at the train station. As he walked down the steps that led away from the station, he noticed Michelle sitting in her car at one of the short-time parking stalls. She smiled and waved to him as their gazes met one another.

Garth opened the passenger door and climbed in. He wasn't sure how many beers he had, but he certainly wasn't feeling any pain. "Thanks for coming to pick me up, Michelle," said Garth.

"I have heard of easing back into the saddle, but going to work for a couple of hours and then spending the whole afternoon in the bar? Are you trying to be the next Ralph Klein?" said Michelle.

Garth let out a half-hearted laugh and said, "No, this morning was horrible. We bought a company called Bear Creek."

Michelle put the car in reverse and waited for some people to walk behind her vehicle before proceeding to back out of the stall. She said, "I saw that. I thought the market liked it as your stock went up five percent after it was announced."

"Well, I guess that depends on your perspective. You see, I did the evaluation of a land sale last year that we lost big time to Bear Creek. I was blamed for not doing an adequate assessment, and now that we bought Bear Creek, it is being brought up again to the point where I had a meeting this morning with the big wigs, and they took turns berating me. To top it all off, numb nuts, Tyler Henderson, was the engineer that did the evaluation of the acquisition. Now they want me to work with numb nuts and learn from him how to 'create value'," said Garth.

"Tyler Henderson?" said Michelle, with a crumpled-up nose. "Blond guy with wild hair?"

"That's the one," said Garth. "Don't tell me you used to go out with him."

"Not me, but Sara did," said Michelle.

"Your roommate Sara?" said Garth. Michelle nodded. "She went out with him for a couple of months. She finally dumped him, as he was never nice to her. He stalked her for a while afterwards. It was so bad that she had to sic her brother on him to get him to leave her alone," said Michelle.

"That would be the same douche," said Garth.

As Michelle drove back to her place, she continued to tell Garth about what she knew about Tyler. "Omar, Sara's wiener dog, didn't care for Tyler at all. When Tyler used to stay over at our place, Omar would find any piece of clothing of his and shit on it. It was so bad that if they locked Omar out of the room, he would just shit in front of the door," said Michelle.

Garth laughed, "Well, like they say, dogs are a great judge of character. I would like to shit on him too." Garth was already feeling in a better mood, but that was customary whenever he was with Michelle.

After a week, Garth had finally made an appointment for himself to meet with Tyler. He had blocked off the whole morning when Tyler had a day available. Tyler was on the floor above Garth, and as Garth walked down the aisle towards Tyler's office, he was reading the nameplates on the office walls and realized he recognized few of the names. When he came to Tyler's office, Tyler was sitting at his desk, typing on his computer. Garth knocked at the door. Tyler never turned to look at him and said, "Gibbins, come in and have a seat. I am just finishing up some e-mails to Ellen and Roger on the progress of our drilling program. It is important that I get this to them as they are doing a road show on the acquisition in Toronto today."

Garth rolled his eyes and sat down in one of the guest chairs. He moved some papers to the side of the cluttered desk so he could set his engineering pad down. Garth looked around Tyler's office. There were papers everywhere, even on the floor. There was a Bachelor of Mechanical Engineering certificate from the University of Waterloo hanging on the wall surrounded by framed pictures of Patrick Roy and Guy Carbonneau. There were no pictures of any family except for a picture of Tyler with some friends holding up beers. A backpack was lying on the floor with clothes hanging half in and half out of it. Garth thought, *this guy is a disaster, no wonder his hair is too.*

When Tyler finished his e-mail, he turned his chair to face Garth. "I didn't think you would ever meet with me," said Tyler.

"Of course. I want to learn about your programs and see if there are any synergies I can use in my area," said Garth. He had struggled to say that, but he put on the bravest face he could manage.

"Okay, where do you want to start?" asked Tyler.

"First off, how much production does the Bear Creek properties make right now?" asked Garth.

"Not much at the moment, but we plan to have production of sixty million cubic feet per day by this time next year, which means we will have four hundred wells on production at that time. With the remaining drilling, we will be able to keep production flat for five years," explained Tyler.

"Wow, that is aggressive. How are you going to be able to get that many wells drilled and on production in that time?" asked Garth.

Tyler continued, "We have secured three dedicated drilling rigs. The leases are all minimal disturbance on native grassland, so it takes no time to get the leases prepared. Spud to rig release for these shallow wells is thirty-six hours. The program is run just like any factory process to maximize time spent on getting wells completed and tied in. Time is money. The faster you can get things done, the cheaper it will be. With this factory process, we can drive down costs by thirty percent. This makes the play highly economic," boasted Tyler.

Garth asked, "What kind of testing do you do? Do you have testers out there?"

Tyler gave a scoff and then he said, "No. That would be too expensive. We record the twenty-four hour shut-in wellhead pressure after perforating, and then we flow the wells back through a choke to an open slop tank. We record the fluid recovery in the tank and based on the pressure at the choke and the size of choke, we calculate a four-hour and twenty-four-hour rate. The government doesn't require anything more and is happy with that for shallow gas."

"What if some of the wells don't test very good. Are there contingencies to change the program?" asked Garth.

"You have to plan for success, Garth. We are confident we can handle wells producing half of what we predict and still be economic," said Tyler.

"I was just wondering as this program is a step out. It might be better to give the wells a longer test to be more confident in their long-term deliverability," said Garth.

"I hate it when people just want to waste money on useless testing when they should be focusing on streamlining the process and driving down costs. That is the difference between you and me. I am focused on creating value, and you are focused on doing science experiments," said Tyler.

Garth sat there and did not say anything. He thought to himself, *There are more differences than that between us and thank God for that.*

"Did we keep any of the operational staff from Bear Creek?" asked Garth.

"No, there was only two contract guys anyways, and we have more than enough people who can look after this," said Tyler.

"Okay," said Garth, "now in predicting the performance of the wells, what method are you applying?"

"We know the volumetric area for each section, and assuming thirty-two wells per section and an ultimate recovery of ninety percent, that gives us two hundred and eight one million cubic feet per well. So what we do is take the average initial rate of two hundred thousand cubic feet and plug it into a decline curve with a harmonic curve for a cumulative of two hundred and seventy five million cubic feet in a fifty year producing life," said Tyler.

Garth took out his calculator as Tyler was talking and did some quick calculations. "That is just under nine Bcf gas of production from each section. That is almost double what we are carrying for reserves on the offsetting lands. Were these reserve estimates verified by our reserve evaluator, Sentinel?"

Tyler laughed, "Sentinel? Those clowns wanted to only give us three and a half Bcf per section with a maximum of twelve wells. They said that thirty-two wells were too many. We used Cody and Montross, who Bear Creek was using. They were much better to work with."

Garth had heard of Cody and Montross before. He remembered what a colleague had told him about which reserve evaluator to use: "If you are buying, use Sentinel. If you are selling, use Cody and Montross."

"From the difference of analysis between the two evaluators, doesn't that give cause for concern?" asked Garth.

Tyler just scoffed. "Garth you are Mr. Pessimist for sure. I bet you always think the glass is half full."

Garth retorted, "Actually, I would prefer to say that the glass was designed to the wrong specifications. You know how to tell a pessimist from an optimist?"

Tyler said, "The difference between you and me."

Garth said, "Well, I suppose. If you place a person in a room full of horse manure, an optimist will climb to the top and start digging. Why? Because with all of this manure, they think there must be a pony somewhere within." Garth paused as he watched the expression on Tyler's face go to one of extreme annoyance. Garth continued, "And you, sir, are covered in horse shit."

Before Tyler could get too mad, Garth cut him off and said, "Seriously, thanks for your time, Tyler. I really appreciate it. I have learned a lot, and I will definitely be applying some of these ideas to my areas."

"No worries, always glad to help show people how it's done, Gibbins," said Tyler.

Garth got up and gathered his engineering pad. He had managed to fill up five pages with notes. Garth had made it a point to write down as much information as possible. From the discussions, he had already found a lot of information that he had to follow up on. The pace at which the program was proceeding was disturbing to him as he pondered if the wells would work out as everyone was betting on.

The next morning, Garth had arranged to meet Terry at one of the Tim Hortons a couple of blocks away from where they worked. The plan was to meet there, as Terry felt it was less likely that someone who worked at Maldere would see them. When Garth arrived, Terry was sitting at a table in the back next to the bathrooms. Terry got up from the table when he saw Garth, and they took their place in line to order their coffees. Garth got his usual with one milk, and Terry always got one milk and three sweeteners. Garth bugged Terry by saying, "C'mon Terry, I think you could stand some sugar to fatten you up. If you turn sideways, you will disappear."

Terry quipped, "Somedays, I wish I could disappear."

They purchased their coffees and returned to the table in the back. As they sat down, Terry said, "So how is every-thing going?"

"It's going," said Garth. "I see that they have been running three rigs on the program, and they are planning to have the compressor station up and running in about three months."

"Have you been able to find out much about how the wells are testing?" asked Terry.

"No. Tyler has been holding that pretty close to his chest. All I get is that they are meeting expectations," said Garth. "Darcy Lowe who used to work in completions is now doing the drilling engineering for the program. I am planning to go out there with him tomorrow and tour the rigs. He also knows the completion consultant as he used to work for him. Darcy has arranged for his consultant to tour me around while they are doing the completions," said Garth.

"That's good. Maybe you can get an idea of how the wells are doing," said Terry.

They both looked up as a man walked by their table to the bathroom. The smell of booze was heavy around him, and as he passed, it hit them like a big wave. The man got to the bathroom door and tried to open it, but it was locked. The man stood there to wait for the person he believed was in there to leave. Terry noticed him standing there and said, "You have to ask one of the workers here to open the electronic lock."

The man blankly stared back at Terry and then he finally moved back to the counter and asked one of the servers to open the door. He then turned to Terry and said, "Thanks man, I might have pissed my pants if I had to wait there."

Terry laughed, "No problem, sir." Then Terry whispered, "By the smell of him, I think it would not be the first time he pissed his pants today."

"I shouldn't laugh, as that will probably be me once Roger gets done with me," said Garth.

"You'll be okay. You're from Saskabush. I know you have been able to hold your liquor since you were twelve," said Terry. "Besides, Roger is going to be over the moon when you save this company from disaster."

Garth didn't say anything as they walked through the door headed back to the office, but he was thinking, *I doubt it.*

The next morning at 6:00 a.m. found Garth pulling into the parking lot of the Crossroads Hotel on Highway 1. He parked beside a new GMC Sierra 4WD pickup that he recognized from hockey and knew it was Darcy's. He transferred his bag containing his safety gear of coveralls, hard hat, steel-toed boots, and safety glasses into Darcy's truck and climbed in. "Morning Darcy. Thanks for giving me the guided tour today," said Garth.

"No problem, young man. It is always good to have company on this drive. Besides, I have a little tidbit of gossip for you," said Darcy.

"About what?" asked Garth.

"Your buddy Tyler there. It just so happens that my girl-friend and I went for a food truck kobasa one day. We decided to go into the Devonian Gardens, as she likes to feed the fish in there. After she had thrown some food in for the fish, we sat down on a bench and ate our lunch. When we were sitting there, we saw Tyler come off the elevator. We were kind of hidden behind a plant, so he did not see us, but he looked like he was waiting for someone. Then from the other elevator came Ellen Sheard. She came up to him, and they embraced in a long, wet kiss. I looked at my girlfriend, and we were like, 'Did you see that?' I thought I was going to upchuck my lunch," said Darcy.

"What? Are you frigging kidding me?" asked Garth incredulously.

"I wish I was. They were there for a couple of minutes, and then they looked around to make sure no one saw them, and left hand in hand," said Darcy.

"Son of a bitch. That explains why she was so cranky to me in that meeting with Maldere. She is doing that little bastard," said Garth.

"So be careful what you say around them as it will get right back to the other and probably to Maldere himself. As years ago, I knew a geologist who had an office next to hers, and Maldere would come down and make frequent 'visits'. She even told him that she was going to screw her way to the top if she had to," said Darcy.

"Jesus Christ, this whole thing gets crazier by the minute," said Garth.

"Truth is stranger than fiction in the oil patch. If I can give you any advice, it is to remember that it is a small world, and the oil patch in Calgary is small indeed. You never know whose boots are under the bed," said Darcy.

They drove on for about a half an hour, and Darcy pulled into a Tim Hortons drive-thru in the Town of Strathmore. Garth was glad he did, as he badly needed his morning caffeine fix. After grabbing their daily dose of Arabica bean blend, they headed back out on to the highway.

"How did you get the name Garth?" asked Darcy. "It is not a real popular name for kids of your vintage."

Garth looked at Darcy. It was a pretty common question that people asked him, and growing up, kids had been relentless in teasing him about it. "It comes from the middle name of my Great Uncle John Garth Gibbins. He was captured during the Dieppe Raid in World War II. He was a prisoner of war for over two years before the camp was liberated by the Russians. His family didn't know if he was dead or alive for many months. He and my grandfather were very close. My dad had decided on the name Garth for me as a tribute to my great uncle," said Garth.

"He was in Dieppe?" asked Darcy.

"Yes. He was part of Cameron Highlanders out of Winnipeg. There actually were quite a few men from Southern Saskatchewan in the Dieppe Raid. They suffered over fifty percent casualties," said Garth.

"Did he ever talk about it much?" asked Darcy.

"A little bit. One story that sticks out in my mind is one he told me as an example of how people can believe in something blindly. He told of a young man from a small town in Saskatchewan where this guy's father was a minister at a United Church. I guess the fellow was famous for not wearing his helmet in exercises when they were training in England. His commanding officers would yell at him constantly. He would just say, 'God will protect me, no need to worry.' My great uncle would say that it would get annoying fast. How he would constantly talk about religion and that he did not have to worry about being killed as God was on his side.

"When that fateful August day finally rolled around, this man was in the same landing craft as my great uncle. Some of the men were throwing up, some were shaking so badly they couldn't move, and some showed no emotion, just looked straight ahead. This guy sat there with his cross pendant in his hand, smiling. He said he would forever remember the look on that fellow's face for as long as he lived. When the gate lowered on the landing craft and it was time to exit, this man stood up in front of my great uncle. Immediately the back of his head exploded when a German round hit him. He fell right in front of my great uncle. He had to jump over his body, and when he looked down at him, he still seemed to be smiling," said Garth.

"Wow, that's horrible," said Darcy.

"Yeah, so my great uncle said blind faith is dangerous. You can deceive your own self into a feeling of invincibility," said Garth. "Other than that, he never talked about it much, at least not to me. I know he told my grandfather a lot more about what happened to him when he was in the war camp. That though they kept to themselves.

"Speaking of blind faith, what are your thoughts on this shallow gas program?" asked Garth.

"Well, for me, one side of it is that I am busy. On the other side though, as a shareholder in Maldere, I am concerned with the amount of money that is being spent without properly validating the assets. We are moving a rig every day. We have all of this activity concentrated in a small area, and I am worried that we are going to have an accident," said Darcy. Garth nodded.

They drove for another two hours on the Number 1 Highway, and then pulled off on to a gravel road that headed south. Beside the highway, where the road started, there were three signs indicating which drilling rigs were drilling down the road. The road was well used and heavily wash boarded. They bounced down the road for about ten minutes and came up over a hill. The hill was about one hundred and fifty feet above the rest of the area. From the crest of the hill, Garth estimated you could see for thirty miles. Maldere called this field Copper Canyon. The name came from the steep-cut riverbanks in the area, where the exposed rock formations of clay and sand radiated a brilliant bronze hue at sunrise and sunset that gave the formations the appearance of copper.

He could see the derricks of three drilling rigs. There was a bunch of pipeline equipment in two different spots that were running the gas pipelines that would tie all the wells in. He could also see numerous big trucks parked at a lease connected with a spiderweb of pipe and hose and knew they must be doing a hydraulic frac on the well. Every direction he looked, there were trucks moving across the prairie and roads. Numerous dust plumes hung in the air, marking the direction that the vehicles moved in. It looked like a war zone.

"I am going to take you to my old Completions Superintendent. His name is Andy Heywood. He is a good man and will be able to show you around. He is overseeing a frac on 14-18 right now," said Darcy. 14-18 stood for a particular well location with respect to the Dominion Land Survey System. Garth was familiar with the survey system being from the farm, but he remembered how hard it was for the kids in his classes from the city to grasp the concept. It was a favourite for the oilfield workers to play tricks on newcomers by giving phony well locations. For convenience, most oil field workers when naming a well location would only use the first two numbers to identify it.

They headed in the direction of the lease that Garth had seen from the hill. They pulled up to the lease, which was clogged with trucks, pumpers, and trailers. Darcy pulled the truck over to the side of the lease road, and they got out and put on their coveralls, hard hats, and boots. Once they had their safety gear on, they made their way to the command centre trailer.

They walked up the grated steps to the door on the command centre and walked in. There were three guys seated in the trailer, watching computer monitors that showed the pressures and rates of the fluid being pumped down the hole. "Darcy. How the hell are ya? Come to hang out with the cool kids, did ya? I thought since you are a driller now, you were too good for our kind," said a man that could only be Andy, Garth guessed. He had greying hair and a big horseshoe moustache. He was a big man, and his coveralls were strained to the point of breaking, especially around the mid-section.

"I will never be too good for you guys," said Darcy.

"And don't you forget it either," said Andy with a grin.

"Andy, please meet Garth," said Darcy.

Garth reached forward, and Andy grabbed Garth's hand and gave it a firm hard shake. Garth looked down at his hand, and it looked so small compared to the big paws of Andy. "So? You are the new gynecologist are you?" said Andy.

Garth just smiled, and said, "Yes." *Gynecologist*? That was a new one. He had been called many things as an engineer, but never that one. Garth had momentarily thought of responding with a derogatory remark to the type of people he was working with, but thought better of it, and only smiled.

They watched the rest of the frack get pumped into the well. As the crew was depressurizing and unhooking the lines, Darcy said, "I will see you guys later. I would love to stay and chat, Andy, but I have to go see how the drilling rigs are making out. I will meet up with you somewhere after lunch."

Andy took Garth around the lease and showed him the equipment that was used to do the hydraulic fracturing. Garth had been around fracking equipment before, but no one had explained it to him as well as Andy. They then climbed into Andy's Dodge pickup truck. It was a white, brand-new truck that was lifted to accommodate the oversized mud tires that had been installed on it. Garth looked at it, and then at Andy.

How was a man of Andy's stature going to be able to climb in that thing? Garth opened the passenger door and climbed onto the running board to hop into the passenger seat. He watched Andy as he opened the driver's door and with a huge strain on the "holy shit" handle on the inside of the truck pulled himself into the seat. With a mighty sigh and a wipe of sweat from his brow, Andy put the truck in gear, and they headed out the lease road.

They drove for a couple of minutes and pulled into another lease. From the wellhead, there was piping running to a rectangular rig tank. Andy parked the truck in front of the wellhead. "This well was fracked this morning. We are flowing the well on clean-up to this rig tank. There is a critical flow prover or what we call a 'rifle nipple' that the gas passes through before entering the tank. Knowing the upstream pressure, temperature, and orifice diameter, we can make a pretty decent estimate of the gas rate. The gas rate we calculate here is what we enter into the completion reports," said Andy.

Garth climbed up the metal steps and peered into the tank. On the opposite side of the tank from where the fluid entered was a pile of frack sand sitting in a couple of feet of water. Every couple of seconds, a blast of gas, water, and sand would exit the nipple and vent into the tank with a loud roar. The concoction would spew for a brief moment into the tank until it stopped and everything fell silent. The fluid could then be heard moving down the pipe, and the process would repeat itself. It reminded Garth of draining an air compressor when the air would spew the condensed water out of the drain.

As Garth watched he said, "How can you tell that the gas rate is accurate with all of this slugging water and sand coming in?"

"It is kind of tough. We take an average pressure upstream and use that to make our calculations. We feel that it is about eighty percent accurate. Good enough for these wells. The zones are going to be commingled anyways, so the rate is trivial," said Andy.

Garth looked on, and then he squinted his eyes and said, "How often do you replace the rifle nipple as the orifice must get washed out with all of this sand passing through it?"

Andy smiled, "I must say, you ask good questions. Most engineers just nod their heads, but I don't think they ever understand any of this. We change out the nipples every five tests or so. If the orifice gets washed out a little bit, it will just mean the well is making more gas than what we are estimating."

Garth didn't say anything further. He was thinking by the looks on how full the tank was, it looked like the well was making more water than gas. If the water was maintaining the pressure at the wellhead, the gas was probably being over estimated by more than one hundred percent. "How much water do you get after these fracks?" asked Garth.

"We usually get seventy-five percent of our load fluid back on these twenty-four hour tests," said Andy.

"You think all of this water is load fluid?" asked Garth.

"Of course. These wells, we are told, don't make much formation water if any at all," said Andy.

Garth brought up his right hand to his face and gave his chin a rub, *Wow! Even the completions guys are drinking the Kool-Aid.*

Garth hung around with Andy for the rest of the morning as they toured the field. They visited the future compression site. The crews were busy with the last stages of connecting the yard piping with the compressors, inlet separator, and dehydrator. Garth estimated they were only weeks away from being ready for start-up. From the gas powered reciprocating engines in front of the compressors, Garth could tell that the machines were going to run on natural gas from the wells themselves.

"Well it is about eleven thirty. Why don't we head over to the Blue Apple Café and have a bite to eat. I am feeling a bit peckish," said Andy.

Garth said, "Sure, sounds good. I am buying. It is the least I could do for you driving me around all day." Garth thought to himself that maybe he would regret this, as it appeared from the size of Andy's paunch he knew what he was doing around a plate of food, and he certainly didn't miss too many opportunities to verify that.

Lunch proved to be pretty uneventful, and Andy did pack the food away, including a huge helping of lemon meringue pie. The meal prices were reasonable, as would be expected in a small town, so Garth did not have to break the bank. Andy told Garth that he grew up in the Peace River region of Northeast British Columbia. His family had homesteaded there in 1918. He had left and went to work in the oil patch when his brothers took over the family farm, as they found they had a hard time working together. He still went back from time to time to help out during seeding and harvesting when he could. Andy and Garth talked a lot about farming and the oil patch as they found they had quite a bit in common.

After lunch, they made the ten-mile trip back to the field. Andy said, "I am going to stop in at Executrix 30. My nephew is working on that rig as the motor man." Executrix 30 was one of the three drilling rigs that had been contracted by Maldere for the drilling of this shallow gas project. Garth knew that the motor man was the second from the bottom of the hierarchy on a drilling rig. The chain of command started at the floor hand to the motor man to the derrick man to the assistant driller and then to the driller. The supervisor was the rig manager. "He has only worked on this rig for a couple of months, but he seems to be catching on pretty good. I worry about him though. My brother would never forgive me if something happened to him," continued Andy.

They pulled on to the lease and parked the truck in front of the office trailer on the drilling rig site. Garth noticed Darcy's truck parked at the trailer as well, so he knew that Darcy was here too. Andy got out and made his way over to the drilling rig. Garth surmised he was going to see his nephew. Garth could see drill pipe standing in the derrick as the crew was tripping pipe out of the hole.

At that moment, Darcy came out of the trailer. "Hey Garth, how is your day going?" asked Darcy.

"Good. It has given me a good understanding of the project and how it is progressing," said Garth. He did not want to get into too many details about how he thought the wells were not being properly tested, as there were too many ears around.

Darcy said, "Good. Hey, I need to get back to Calgary to get my kids ready for soccer tonight as my wife is going to be held up at work. Are you ready to head back?"

Garth knew he had seen enough and nodded his head. "Yeah, we can head back. I am just going to say good-bye to Andy and thank him for everything," said Garth.

"I will come with you," said Darcy. They both walked over to the rig and thanked Andy. After watching the crew trip pipe for a few stands, they climbed back into Darcy's truck and started the trek back into Calgary.

Chapter 6

The next few weeks passed with Garth and Terry unable to find an audience that wanted to listen to what they had found in support of slowing down the project. It was the start of summer holidays, which meant it was also time for Stampede week. This was notoriously a difficult time to get business done. Prior to moving to Calgary, Garth had watched the Stampede Parade and rodeo on television. What he did not know from watching it on TV was how it was a huge ten-day party. It enveloped the whole city and its people. There were free pancake breakfasts all over town, and everyone wore Western wear. Even the top brass at the companies would set aside their normal suits and ties for cowboy boots, blue jeans, and cowboy hats. One of the highlights for many of the normal working stiffs was the Corporate Stampede Party.

These parties were famous for over indulgences in drinking and carnal sin. So much so that it is noted that in the weeks following Stampede week there is an appreciable increase in divorces, STDs, and nine months later, baby births. The Maldere Stampede Party was one of the most infamous. This year it was to be held at the outdoor tent that the Sorrel Horse set out in its parking lot and which could accommodate a couple of thousand people.

The morning of the Maldere Stampede Party found Garth and his coffee gang – Ken, Mike, and Brady – en route to the Sorrel Horse tent. None of them had worked more than ten minutes that day as they had spent most of the morning at one of the fracking company's pancake breakfasts. There they had enjoyed ample quantities of pancakes and "frack juice". Frack juice was simply gin and orange juice, but they had drunk plenty of it. They walked up to the entrance of the tent where some of the Maldere organizing committee were handing out wristbands and two complimentary drink tickets to each staff member.

There were two bars set up at each end of the tent and numerous beer tubs with good-looking hostesses manning each one. The beer tubs were galvanized steel stock tanks that were normally used for watering livestock. These tubs were full of ice and ice-cold bottles of beer, water, and coolers. Ken and Garth headed to the closest tub, which was being staffed by a beautiful young blonde-haired woman. She wore a black belly shirt that had Sorrel Horse Saloon written across it underneath her exposed cleavage, along with tight, cut-off jean shorts and brown leather chaps. They both grabbed a tall, cold Corona from the young lady, gave her the tickets, and turned to observe the crowd.

Garth surveyed the scene before him. There were people everywhere. It always amazed him how all these people worked for the same company as he did. He swore he had never even seen some of them before. He noticed even his boss Dave was there, and Garth thought how silly he looked in a cowboy hat, as it did not fit him at all. This was Stampede though and nobody would care. Besides, no one would say anything because he was a boss. Mike and Brady rejoined them after they had grabbed their rye and cokes from the bar. "Let's see what shenanigans will happen this year. I bet 'ole Dave will hook up with some young girl in accounting again like he did last year. How any of those girls will have anything to do with that old bastard is beyond me," said Mike.

Ken shrugged and said, "He has money and power. That can cover a lot of age spots."

They noticed two young ladies headed their way, and Ken said, "Watch out, Brady, here comes Amanda." The one lady was Amanda Wilkinson, who worked in the land department. At every company function, after she had taken on a jag of alcohol, she would search out Brady. Amanda was a full-figured girl with a beautiful, round face topped with long, black hair. She was very attractive; however, she had a tendency to over-indulge at these gatherings. "Well here looks like a bunch of trouble," said Amanda.

"No trouble here, Amanda. We believe in being part of the party but not being the party," said Ken.

"Boys, this is Lisa McNichol. She started in the land department a couple of months ago. Lisa these are the coffee boys: Ken, Mike, Garth, and this one is Brady," said Amanda as she wrapped her arm around Brady's. "Come on, Brady, let's go dance. Mike you can dance with Lisa," said Amanda. Mike and Brady looked at each other and guzzled their rye and cokes and headed off to the dance floor arm in arm with Amanda and Lisa.

The country music was blaring, and there were only a handful of patrons on the dance floor. It was still early in the afternoon, but they didn't care. "Mike looks like he is made of wood out there," said Ken. "Lisa is probably wishing upon a star to turn him into a real boy." Garth couldn't help it, and when he burst out laughing, he sprayed out a mouthful of beer.

"Gibbins, do I need to get you a towel?" came a voice from behind them. Garth cringed. He recognized that voice immediately. He turned to make a snappy comeback to Tyler. When he did though, he was surprised to be looking into the pretty face of Cathleen Leslie who was standing beside Tyler. Her red hair was tied into pigtails, and she wore a Western shirt that was tied off at her belly button and skin-tight blue jeans.

Garth was speechless for a moment. Ignoring Tyler completely, he managed to say, "Hi Cathleen. Sorry, Ken here has good timing to always say something funny right when I am taking a swig of beer."

Cathleen said, "When doesn't he have something funny to say."

Tyler just scoffed and said, "We are getting a drink. Anybody want something?"

Garth held up his almost empty beer and said, "Sure, that would be great, thanks."

"I will come with you. I have to piss my dink any way," said Ken.

When Ken and Tyler had walked away, Garth said, "Are you and Tyler seeing each other?"

Cathleen smiled and said, "We went on a few dates, but I don't think Tyler can have feelings for someone other than himself. We are just friends. He actually is kind of fun to be around, but he is too self-centred for my taste. I prefer a man who is confident but not that full of himself."

Garth said, "Thank goodness. You deserve someone way better than him."

"Who did you have in mind, Garth?" asked Cathleen with a sheepish grin. "I had always thought of you. But I hear that you have a girlfriend now." Garth could feel his face getting hot, and he knew it wasn't because of the heat of the sun. He was blushing.

"Yes. I have been seeing a girl for a couple of months now," said Garth.

"Who is she?" asked Cathleen.

"Michelle Newfield. She works at Huntoon Oil and Gas," said Garth.

"She is a lucky girl. I would like to meet her," said Cathleen.

"She is coming here this afternoon later on, so you probably will," said Garth.

"Well, in the meantime, let's go dance," said Cathleen. Before Garth could react, Cathleen grabbed his hand and led him out onto the dance floor.

Cathleen spent the afternoon hanging out with Garth and his friends. From time to time, Garth would look around and see Tyler's eyes burning into him. Garth wanted to tell Cathleen about what Darcy had told him about Darcy and Ellen Sheard, but he couldn't bring himself to do it. He was having so much fun with her that he wasn't sure how she would react.

At about 5:00 in the afternoon, Garth was waiting for Michelle by the main entrance. After 5:00 p.m., significant others were allowed to come into the Corporate party. Garth saw her come walking up. She looked amazing in her purple Western shirt, tight blue jeans, and a straw Budweiser cowboy hat. She saw him immediately and ran towards him. He wrapped his arms around her and gave her a kiss. "Whoa, there big fella, you are going to break me. How many drinks have you had?" asked Michelle.

"I have no idea," said Garth. "It only takes one beer to get me drunk." Michelle frowned and looked into Garth's bloodshot brown eyes. Garth continued, "And that one beer is number fourteen, I think."

Michelle laughed. "Come on, mister fourteen beers. Introduce me to some of your colleagues."

Just then Cathleen came up to the two of them. "You must be Michelle. I have heard a lot about you," said Cathleen.

Garth paused and said, "Michelle this is Cathleen. She is a Geologist I work with."

"Hi Cathleen," said Michelle. Garth could see Michelle looking Cathleen up and down with a distrustful eye. This was making Garth feel very uncomfortable.

As they stood there talking, Peter Bozak came up behind them and placed his arm around Cathleen. "What a lovely scene we have here. How is everyone doing?" said Peter. Cathleen had a look of disgust and rolled her eyes as she lowered her shoulder to get Peter's arm off of her. She walked over and stood beside Garth and turned to look back at Peter. This did not phase Peter. In fact, it seemed to please him, as if that was the response he was hoping to get. "Garth. Have you managed to get your drilling program figured out for this year or have you been too busy chasing skirts?" asked Peter with a sickly twisted grin.

"I have been busy doing whatever is necessary, and right now it is necessary that I get these girls a drink. Talk to you later Pete," replied Garth. With that, he grabbed each girl by the arm and turned around and headed as far away as possible from Peter.

"Hey Cathleen. Tyler was looking for you," called out Peter as they walked away.

"That guy gives me the creeps most of the time. When he is drinking, he totally freaks me out. He is always laying his stinking hands on me," said Cathleen.

"Yeah, he can be an ass when he is drinking. Ordinarily he is harmless," said Garth.

"Well you know what the Latins say, *in vino veritas,* meaning 'in wine there is truth'. If you want to know a person's true inner personality, observe how they are when they are drunk. They will reveal their true self. If the guy is an ass when drunk, he is an ass through and through. When he is sober, he is only pretending to hide it," said Michelle.

Cathleen nodded. "So, what would you say I am showing about my true self right now? I have had a beer or maybe ten," said Garth.

"Well, from my careful observations, I would say that deep down you are funny, kind-hearted, and fun loving," said

Michelle as she wrapped an arm around him and pulled her body close to his.

"Ha, I know a few people who would disagree with that," said Garth.

After a couple of hours, Garth was losing steam fast. He had been drinking most of the day in the hot sun. Michelle noticed this, and when Cathleen had left them to go to the bathroom, she said, "How about I take you home now?"

Garth gave her a drunken look and said, "I am ready." Michelle snatched up Garth's arm and guided him through the crowd, out the exit. There was only a small percentage of people from Maldere left, and the bar was filling up quickly with other Stampede goers.

They walked out of the bar and onto the sidewalk. The streetlights were on, and the last rays of sunlight were disappearing over the tall buildings of downtown. There were only a handful of people on the street, as most were inside the various bars along the street. Loud music and people shouting and hollering could be heard up and down the street. They walked past a pair of police officers on pedal bikes as they patrolled down 8th Avenue. Michelle had parked her car in a parkade a few blocks away, and they walked slowly towards the parkade.

They were only a block away as they passed a dark alley that ran behind two buildings. They could hear someone yelling profanity in the alley, and then they heard the sickening sound of a fist striking flesh and bone. Garth and Michelle peered into the alley. Two young men were standing over a slumped figure and were each delivering kicks to the motionless body on the ground. "Hey! Get away from him!" screamed Michelle. The two young men looked back at Garth and Michelle, then turned and ran out the other side of the alley.

Michelle ran up to the man lying on the pavement. He was in the fetal position, motionless, and had blood trickling from his nose and ear. Michelle was first to arrive and stooped down to the injured man as Garth slowly staggered up to them. He looked down at the man and recognized the bloody face immediately. It was Tyler Henderson. Many thoughts were running through Garth's alcohol fogged mind. So much so, he just stood there and swayed back and forth for a moment. "Oh my God, Garth. It's Tyler," cried Michelle. "He is unconscious, but he is breathing. We need to get him an ambulance." Garth couldn't believe it. He had often wanted to punch out Tyler but seeing him like this with a bloodied mess of a face was a sobering thought.

"Garth, go see if you can find those police officers we passed." Garth looked at her, blinked blankly, and then said, "I am not leaving you here in case those guys come back."

"Don't worry about me. I don't think those guys will be back, and Tyler needs our help. You can do this," said Michelle.

Garth straightened up and ran back to where the alley met the street. He looked down both ways and saw the officers were two blocks down, talking with some patrons that were on the street. Garth knew that in his alcohol-induced condition he was not going to be able to run down there. There were three women who were walking towards Garth and were in between him and the officers. Garth yelled at the women, "Hey! Can you get the officers down there? There is an injured man in the alley here, and he needs an ambulance." The women stopped and stared at Garth for a moment. Garth knew they were thinking that this was a ruse of some sort. Finally, one of the women turned and ran back to officers.

Garth watched as the woman ran up to the officers and saw her point down to Garth's direction. Garth waved and the officers jumped on their bikes and pedalled towards him. Once Garth was satisfied that the officers were on their way, he headed back to Michelle and Tyler. He was quite intoxicated, but he could feel himself sobering up by the minute. "They are coming," said Garth.

"Thank goodness. Who would do such a thing?" said Michelle. Garth thought to himself that he could have at one time. Many a time when Tyler was in front of him, he had thought, *If I hit him right now, he would never expect it. I could just lay him out.* But seeing Tyler lying there before him now, Garth felt ashamed he had ever had those thoughts.

The policemen rode up to them. "What happened?" said one of the officers. The officer was in his early twenties with short brown hair and a British accent.

"We heard a commotion in the alley and saw two men laying the boots to him. We yelled at them and they ran out that way," said Michelle. The other officer, who was older, was a tall Black Canadian who pulled out his handheld radio and called for police back-up and an ambulance.

It took only minutes for an ambulance to pull up to the scene. Garth watched as two paramedics, a man and a woman, raced out of the ambulance and opened the back door. They wheeled the gurney over to Tyler's immobile body. The woman bent down to Tyler and initiated a review of his vitals. Garth in his drunken state was trying to comprehend the scene playing out before him. It felt surreal and as if he were watching this through someone else's eyes.

The paramedics loaded Tyler onto the wheeled stretcher and placed him into the ambulance. The ambulance took off with the sirens blaring. Garth watched it go as onlookers were gathering around the entrance to the alley. The onlookers were being held back by officers, who had been called in to secure the crime scene.

The older officer wrote down Garth and Michelle's statements. "Thank you. If it weren't for you coming upon the gentleman when you did, this would be a murder investigation. He is by no means out of the woods yet, but because of you he has a fighting chance," said the officer. He handed Michelle a business card and continued. "If you think of anything else after you get home, no matter how small the detail, please let me know. Now get this one home and try to get some sleep," he said as he gestured his thumb at Garth.

Michelle thanked the officer and then said, "Do you know what hospital he will be taken to?"

"Foothills, most likely," replied the officer.

Michelle and Garth walked the rest of the way to her car. They drove back to Garth's place in silence, neither one able to grasp what they had just witnessed. Garth was coming down from his beer high and now was feeling extremely tired and only wanted to go to bed. Michelle made sure he drank a couple of glasses of water before retiring. She said it would make him feel better in the morning, as he wouldn't be so dehydrated. After forcing the water down, Garth stripped down to his underwear and flopped down on his bed. Now that he was lying down, he felt a bad case of vertigo and the room was spinning. He did an old trick that a friend had told him of placing one foot on the wall to help with the spinning sensation. The wall felt cold to his foot, and before Michelle had climbed into bed, he was snoring loudly.

The next morning, Garth and Michelle slept in as long as they could. Surprisingly to Garth he actually felt pretty good. *Maybe there is something in the water after all,* he thought. He got to the office about 9:30. He walked onto his floor and noticed from the motion detection lights in each office that most of the offices were vacant this morning as the offices were dark. They were most likely at a pancake breakfast somewhere or were hung over, guessed Garth. There was one office that had a light on, and Garth's mood sank as it was Big Dave's. Garth wondered if Dave had heard about Tyler, so he decided to walk up to Dave's door and knock.

Dave looked up from his desk. His face was pale, and his eyes were red. Garth wasn't sure if it was because he was hung over or if he had gotten some bad news, possibly about Tyler.

"Garth, come in and have a seat. I know you just got here, so you probably have not heard yet. Tyler was badly assaulted last night. It appears he suffered severe head trauma, and he is currently in an induced coma until some of the swelling on his brain goes down," said Dave.

Garth nodded his head and said, "I know." He didn't feel like telling Dave that he and Michelle were the ones who had found him. "From what I understand, the doctors are unsure if he is going to make it. Regardless, he is not going to be back to work anytime soon. Since you are the one most familiar with the program in his area, I want you to look after it until Tyler is well enough to return," said Dave.

"Sure," said Garth. Dave looked into Garth's eyes with that soul-piercing stare of his and said, "This program means a lot to Maldere, and we need it to be successful. There are a lot of eyes on it, so do your best not to mess it up. Make sure to check your ego at the door and follow the company line. It is in your best interest as well that the program succeeds."

Garth was taken aback by that statement. *My ego? Are you frigging kidding me?* he thought. Garth stood up and looked back at the ashen little man that sat before him and said, "I will do whatever needs to be done." He did not wait for a response and walked out of Dave's office into his own.

Garth sat at his desk contemplating everything that had gone on in the last twenty-four hours. His biggest nemesis was lying at death's door, and he had helped save him from certain death. Now he was going to look after Tyler's main project and knew there would be hell to pay once Tyler found out and returned to work. That is, if he survived. All kinds of thoughts were running through his head when a familiar face walked through his office door.

"Gibbers, did you hear about Tyler?" said Ken McAdams. Garth looked up from his computer screen and at Ken's big frame filling Garth's doorway.

"Come on, there are too many ears here. Let me buy you a coffee, and I will fill you in on what I know," said Garth. He got up and led Ken down the hallway to the elevator.

Chapter 7

Two weeks later found Garth working hard to keep up to date with the drilling program. He had to review the logs from the wells and pick the intervals in the wells that would be perforated and fracture stimulated. He also had to keep track of the flow tests in order to ensure they were on track to match the production estimates. More than fifty wells had been drilled, completed, and tested since the start of the program. These wells had pipelines connected to them to flow the gas to the compressor station. Tensions were tight. Today was the day that the compressor station was to be started, and they would get the first indications of how much gas would be produced from the wells.

The compressors were to be started at 9:00 a.m., and Garth was waiting by his phone to get a call from the field foreman, Ted Horgan. Ted was due to give an update on how everything was running. Big Dave had already come into Garth's office twice to check on any news of how the wells were producing. Finally, at about 9:50 a.m., Garth's office phone rang. Garth looked at the call display on his phone and saw from the three-digit prefix that the call was coming from the field. Garth answered the phone with, "Good morning, Garth Gibbins speaking."

"Garth, how are you this morning? Ted here. We have one of the compressors up and running. We had a few issues getting it going, as the inlet separator was flooded. I am not sure what that is about. Maybe there was water left in some of the pipelines after pressure testing. We seem to have got it figured out now as we have been running at about two hundred and sixty thousand cubic metres per day. We will slowly drop the suction pressure, but it seems to be running good where it is," said Ted.

Garth quickly did the conversion in his head; two hundred and sixty thousand cubes was just under ten million cubic feet per day. This was a calculation he had to do often as the field would use the metric system since that is how they had to record the production to the government. However, the office would use imperial to report the numbers to shareholders, who many were American. "Wow, that is pretty good. That means we are doing about two hundred thousand cubic feet per day per well," said Garth.

"Yeah, about five cubes a well," said Ted.

"Is there water still coming into the separator?" asked Garth.

"Yes. There is still some trickling in, but it seems to be levelling off," said Ted.

"Okay, let's keep an eye on that. If you get the chance, I would like to know the flowing pressures at the wells. Then I can check the pressures in the field to make sure we don't have any big pressure drops through the pipelines. The pressure drops would tell us if we have water holdup in any of the lines," said Garth. "Fantastic job on getting everything started up, and I am glad to hear it is running well. I will pass this along to management here. Thanks again Ted," said Garth.

"Glad to help, and I will get someone to check the pressures. If I run into any problems, I will give you a ring," said Ted.

"Good, we will talk to you later," said Garth.

"Right O. Bye Garth," said Ted.

As Garth hung up the phone, he could see that Big Dave was already in his doorway. "So, is it doing better than you thought?" said Dave. He had a cat that swallowed the canary look on his face, and any positive thoughts that Garth had were quickly erased. It was apparent he had been eavesdropping on the conversation.

"We are making about ten million cubic feet per day from fifty wells. They had some issues with water at the inlet separator that is peculiar, but I am getting more information on that. But yes, it looks good right now," said Garth.

"See, all of your ranting and raving about the sky following was all for not," said Dave.

Garth did not drop his eyes from Dave's and narrowed them a bit as he said, "It is still early yet. The interference I am worried about will show up in the months to come."

"Ah, you people who always look for rain in every cloud," said Dave. "I will let the rest of senior management know." He turned around and walked out the door.

Garth shook his head and mumbled under his breath, "Don't forget some mouthwash and knee pads, you ass-kissing bastard."

Later on that day after the stock market had closed, a news release from Maldere was sent out. The release stated that production had been initiated on the property that was bought from Bear Creek. It was e-mailed to all of the Maldere employees as well. Garth was busy reading the news release when he came across a statement that made him cringe: *Based on the initial success, Maldere is planning to accelerate the drilling program in the Copper Canyon field. The company expects to have three hundred wells on production by the end of the year with associated production of sixty million cubic feet per day from these Bear Creek assets.*

The release continued that Maldere was bringing in two more drilling rigs to hit the target of three hundred wells by the end of the year. It was anticipated that there was enough well inventory to keep all five rigs busy for at least two years. Garth put his head down and rested his head on his hands covering his eyes. *Oh my God,* he thought.

A knock at the door made Garth look up. It took a moment for his eyes to adjust from being pressed closed by his hands. Darcy Lowe was standing in his doorway. "Doing some sort of meditation, Garth?" asked Darcy.

"I was hoping I could make this news release disappear if I concentrated hard enough," said Garth.

"Yeah, I read that. Pretty aggressive program. Are you sure you can do that?" asked Darcy.

"I think it will be easier to lasso a unicorn," said Garth, shaking his head.

"Well, you must have had some input into the news release, didn't you? asked Darcy.

"I gave Dave an update when the compressor came online. Other than that, nobody has said a word to me," said Garth.

"Oh. So, I better sell my shares is what you're telling me?" asked Darcy.

"I would hold off doing that for a couple of weeks. I am sure the stock price will go up after this release. Give it a couple of weeks, and if it were me, I would sell everything I own," said Garth. Darcy just smiled. Garth wasn't sure if Darcy thought he was joking, but Garth was dead serious.

"Anyhow, I went and saw Tyler at the hospital," said Darcy.

"How is he doing?" asked Garth.

"His face is still quite swollen and bruised. You would hardly recognize him. His family has said he is making progress through his therapy. At first, I guess, he really struggled finding words or the ability to form sentences. When he struggles with that he becomes frustrated and angry. That is expected though with serious brain injuries. They said it is a long process for the brain to recover, and he most likely will never get back to one hundred percent. His family is just thankful that he is alive, and they would really like to talk to you and thank you. So, if you could, I think it would be a good idea if you went and paid him a visit," said Darcy.

"I was planning on going in the next couple of days. I was just waiting to give them some space until he got further down the road to recovery," said Garth. He didn't tell Darcy, but in reality, he was scared and apprehensive about seeing Tyler this way and especially Tyler's family.

"That would be great. I know you were not his biggest fan, and I find it ironic that you were responsible for saving him. I am proud of you. I think we could all learn from that," said Darcy. Darcy shook Garth's hand and gave it a firm grip. Then he looked deep into Garth's brown eyes and said, "Just make sure you go see him. I think it will be good for everyone. Even you," said Darcy. As Garth watched Darcy leave, his eyes caught the painting in the hall. *In my wildest dreams, I never expected a storm like this,* thought Garth.

Two days later found Garth and Michelle entering the sliding entrance doors of the Foothills Hospital. That old sickening hospital smell that Garth disliked so much wafted into his nostrils as they entered the atrium. The floors had just been polished, and the lights glared and reflected from off the tile. His rubber-soled shoes made a squeaking noise as he walked across the floor. When they arrived at Tyler's room, Garth felt his heart in his throat, and he had a tingly feeling in his hands and feet. A part of him was hoping that Tyler or his family would not be there. But when he looked into the room, he could see Tyler sitting up in his bed. The others in the room, Garth assumed, were Tyler's mom, dad, and little brother. His little brother was a miniature carbon copy of Tyler except instead of the shock of blond hair that Tyler had, his brother's hair was quite brown.

Tyler's mom and dad turned in their chairs to see who had entered. Garth guessed they had heard his shoes coming from fifty feet away. Tyler's mom's face lit up, and she jumped to her feet and ran to Michelle. She hugged Michelle tightly and tears started to run down her face. She was an attractive lady in her mid-fifties, but her beautiful face on this day was showing the effects of worry and lack of sleep. "Thank you so much for saving our Tyler. We are so thankful he had friends such as you that came across him when you did," said Tyler's mom.

She then turned and gave Garth a huge hug. Garth felt like his ribs were going to poke out of the back of his shirt. "Thank you so much," she continued and gave Garth a huge kiss on his cheek. "I know I have not met you before, but I recognize your picture from the newspaper. Forgive me, but I am so thankful for what you did. I am Sandy, Tyler's mom, and this is Martin, Tyler's dad, and our youngest son Mitch," said Sandy. Martin shook Garth's hand and then gave Michelle a hug as well.

"Tyler, honey, this is Garth and Michelle. They were the ones who helped get you to the hospital after your accident," said Sandy. Tyler looked at the two of them and a smile came to his lips and he said, "The hockey player." Garth smiled and felt tears starting to fall down his face. Tyler's face was still badly swollen, and Garth had to look hard at him to confirm that this was Tyler. It was unbelievable to see someone so strong and confident looking so frail and vulnerable. Garth swiped away the tears and said, "Hey Tyler. Good to see you up and at 'em."

Tyler slapped his hand on the mattress beside him and motioned Garth to sit there. Garth hesitated, but then he sat down beside Tyler. Tyler then wrapped his arms around Garth and gave him a hug. He settled close beside Garth and held on to his arm. This made Garth uncomfortable. He was not expecting anything like this at all. They sat and made small conversation about how Tyler's recovery was going. Tyler would interrupt quite often, but all he seemed to want to talk about was hockey. He never said Garth's name, but he certainly remembered him. Not from work though, but from playing hockey.

"It is going to be a tough road, but it is great to see how Tyler is advancing each day," said Sandy.

"That is good to hear. He is a great guy, and we can't wait to see him make a full recovery," said Michelle.

Before Garth knew what he was saying, he said, "Yes, we can't wait to see him back at work being his old self." Garth felt embarrassed and ashamed as he said it. He had often felt such bad feelings towards Tyler. Now seeing him like this with his family concerned with his well being made Garth feel like a heel. "Has he had many visitors from Maldere?" asked Garth.

"A few people that he worked with and a couple of the big wigs came in one day," said Martin.

"I believe it was Maldere, Kane, and Shaw. Isn't that right, honey?" said Martin.

"That's right," said Sandy. "Ellen Sheard wasn't here?" asked Garth.

"Not that I know of. Who is she?" asked Sandy.

Garth had thought for sure Ellen would have come to see Tyler; especially if they were lovers, you would think she would have been concerned for his health. Garth thought quickly. He couldn't blurt out "because she was doing him", so he said, "She is our VP of Exploration, and usually she follows those other three to everything it seems."

Sandy and Martin just looked at him with a look that said, "Oh I see." They then went back to talking about the other visitors that Tyler had. Garth and Michelle only stayed for about another ten minutes as Tyler was starting to get tired and agitated. They said good-bye, and the Hendersons thanked and hugged Garth and Michelle again.

Tyler gave Garth a thumbs-up and said, "See you, Gibbs." Garth paused; he had never heard Tyler call him anything other than by his last name, Gibbins.

As Garth and Michelle walked back to the parking lot to Garth's truck, Michelle said, "What was that about Ellen Sheard?"

Garth did not answer right away as he was deciding if he should tell Michelle the truth or not. Finally, he thought it would be best to let Michelle in on what he knew. "Well, I have it on good authority that Ellen was screwing Tyler," said Garth.

"What do you mean? She was trying to play with his career?" said Michelle.

"No, I mean like she was playing slap and tickle with him," said Garth.

"So?" said Michelle.

"She is our VP of Exploration, and she is about twice his age," said Garth.

"Again. So?" said Michelle. "Why does that make any difference to you?"

That was not the response Garth was expecting. "I think that's why she is so hard on me," said Garth. "She is protecting her boyfriend."

Michelle smiled. "I think you are too paranoid. Not everyone is out to get you or involved in some conspiracy. Maybe they are in love." Garth looked back at her, tilted his head, and rolled his eyes.

The weeks passed and Garth remained busy at work. New wells were coming on weekly, and the production from Copper Canyon had climbed to twenty million cubic feet per day. However, there was some cause for concern as the last few wells that had been brought on production did not appear to add to the production total. Garth had left a message to Ted Horgan to investigate on why the production was not climbing.

Garth's phone rang, and by the call display he could see it was Ted. "Hi Ted. How is it going this morning?" asked Garth.

"Well, it could be better," said Ted.

"Oh, so what were you able to find out?" asked Garth.

"Okay, so first we found five wells on the 9-26 leg that have no pressure on them. We had the gas tester out on the wells, and he hooked up his flow meter to the gas taps and there was no pressure there. Nothing, not even a fart," explained Ted.

Garth pulled up his well tracking spreadsheet and asked, "You said the 9-26 leg?"

"Yes. It has five wells on it," said Ted.

Garth double-checked his sheet and then said, "Well, I know why there is no pressure on those wells. Those wells have not been completed yet."

"Seriously? How could that have happened?" asked Ted.

Garth could detect the frustration in his voice. Garth said, "I will have to check with Cody Kramer, the pipeline coordinator, to see why they tied those wells in. They were not on the schedule to be tied in."

"Son of a bitch. Alright, some other things that we found is that the wells in the south legs are making quite a bit of fluid. We found some of the wells had little pressure on them, so we sent a swabbing rig over to see if we could find any water in them. On a couple of wells, we pulled nine cubic metres of water out of them, and the water was still coming," said Ted.

"Wait how much? Did you say nine?" asked Garth. Garth pulled out his calculator and began punching in numbers.

"Yes, nine cubes," said Ted.

"A wellbore with four-and-a-half-inch casing down to total depth should only hold about six cubes," said Garth. "That means that the well is flowing a pretty high rate of water." Garth had known that water was going to be an issue on the wells to the south, but even he had not expected it to be this bad.

"We also retested some of the first wells we tied in last month, and they are down about fifty percent of what they first tested at," said Ted.

"Yeah, that is not surprising. These wells that are fracture stimulated usually have steep declines," said Garth.

"Also, we checked some pressure drops in the field, and it looks like we are seeing some high pressure drops in some of the lines," said Ted.

"Can we send pigs down the lines to push down the lines?" asked Garth.

"Unfortunately, we can't easily do that as pig senders or receivers weren't put on most of the lines to save money. Besides we were told these wells wouldn't make any water," said Ted. Pigs were commonly made from urethane or polyurethane and sort of resembled a bullet. They were designed to be pushed down the line by pressure differential to push out the liquids. The name "pig" came to be as the original pigs were made from straw wrapped in wire that made a squealing noise that sounded like a pig as they travelled through the pipe.

Garth took everything in that Ted was telling him, and he was thinking about what he was going to do now. He had to try to get the brakes put on the drilling program, as it felt everything was spiralling out of control. He had written down everything Ted had relayed to him, and after he hung up with Ted, Garth got up and walked over to Big Dave's office.

Garth knocked on the door, and Big Dave waved him in. "Garth, how is everything going? What kind of production is Copper Canyon making today?" asked Dave. Garth noted the big smile on Dave's lips and knew that after what Garth had to tell him that smile was not going to last for long.

Garth reported on the conversation he had with Ted. Dave listened attentively, and Garth watched that smile turn into an evil snarl. When Garth had finished, Dave looked directly at Garth and said, "Did we complete the right intervals in the wells?"

Garth was trying to hold himself back from getting too defensive and said, "We completed the same intervals that were completed by Bear Creek or what we complete in our own offsetting lands."

"Well, obviously you have completed these wells incorrectly for them to be making this much water. You need to go back and check your intervals and change how you are picking them to get the gas back and shut off this water," said Dave.

Garth knew he had a terrible poker face and could feel his face turning red. "If you remember the boardroom meeting, I said this is a deep basin gas trap, and as you move south, you are going to get more water and less gas. That is why I did not want to have this aggressive of a program. It needs a slow and easy approach," seethed Garth.

"Young man, I am well aware of what you said. Are you now sabotaging this program to serve a point?" glared Dave.

"I am a shareholder too, and believe me, I want to do what is best for this company, just the same as you. Faced with this new information we have to slow down the program. At the very least, we need to stop drilling the wells in the southern part of Copper Canyon," pleaded Garth.

"There will be no slowing down of the program. We have already presented this program, and we can't change it, especially right after we just released it. Now go back and look through the wells that have been completed and make the appropriate changes to fix them," said Dave.

"Fine I will, but I am going to need to spend more money. I would like to suggest running down-hole cameras to confirm where the water is coming from on some of the wells we have done," said Garth.

"What? That is too expensive and besides that doesn't work," sneered Dave.

"It will only cost six thousand dollars per well. How can you say that it doesn't work? It is a video of fluid entering the well. Isn't a picture supposed to be worth a thousand words?" retorted Garth.

"I hate it when people just want to waste money," said Dave.

"So do I, and I am trying to spend a little money to stop from wasting a huge pile of it," replied Garth.

"Fine. Have it your way, if it pleases you," said Dave.

Garth was no longer nervous or defensive. He had switched into full-on annoyed gear now. He said, "Since you feel I have been selecting the wrong interval, why don't you pick the intervals on the next twelve wells, and we will see how they compare to the ones I have done."

Dave was getting fully irritated by this time. Without giving it a further thought, he said, "I will show you what you have been doing wrong. Now until you get all of this straightened out, don't be telling anyone about the results. We don't need a chicken little running around saying that the sky is falling on the ambiguous results of a few wells."

"It is more than just a few wells," said Garth.

"Whatever. Now you have got a lot of work to do, so you better get to it. And remember this stays between us," said Dave as he waved his hand indicating it was time for Garth to leave.

Garth smiled and sped out of Dave's office. Garth felt his blood boiling, but instead of blowing his top, he realized that he was no longer afraid of Dave. He actually saw him as a scared animal, and he actually felt sorry for him in a weird kind of way.

Garth got back to his office and sat at his desk. He wanted to tell someone about what was going on, but he felt a shadow of a doubt about his assessment of the Copper Canyon project. Was Dave right in some way? That Garth had already had the perceived notion that the program was not going to succeed?

Did he have a biased opinion of how it was going to play out, and he was setting it up for failure? He decided he was going to step back and truly re-evaluate the results with fresh eyes before he took this to Terry.

Weeks passed and one day Garth found himself walking through the Plus 15 that connected the Maldere building with the shopping centre complex of downtown Calgary. The Plus 15 is a pedestrian skywalk system that features covered walkways between many of the buildings downtown. It was called Plus 15 as most of the walkways are 15 feet above the street level. The covered walkways were great, especially when there was inclement weather outside, as it provided a heated and dry path that a pedestrian could follow from practically one end of downtown to the other. Today, Garth was heading back from a doctor's appointment he had in another part of the downtown. There were some sidewalk repairs being done on the street, and Garth had opted for the Plus 15 to bypass the construction area.

Garth was walking fast as he wanted to get to work as quickly as possible to check in on the progress of the Copper Canyon project. He had been working hard gathering information on the new wells and their performance. His recent analysis supported his hypothesis from the work he had done early on. The wells were being drilled too close to one another, and there was little gas to be found as the program continued to the south. From the down-hole camera work, he found that water was coming into the wellbore from all three zones; however, the worst offenders were the Milk River and Medicine Hat formations. Something that gave Garth great amusement was the fact that the wells where Big Dave had picked the completion intervals were worse than the average. Something had to be done immediately, or Maldere was at risk of severely over-capitalizing the Copper Canyon program.

Garth looked up and saw Amanda and Lisa walking towards him. They had solemn looks on their faces, and when they saw Garth, they ventured right up to him. "Sorry to hear about the accident on the rig," said Amanda. Lisa looked on with a sympathetic look.

Garth was puzzled, "What accident?" he said.

Amanda frowned and said, "You haven't heard?" Garth shook his head. "Oh, I am so sorry to be the first one to tell you, but a young man died on a rig early this morning, and I think it was in your area," said Amanda.

Garth had an anxious feeling, and his head felt like it was swimming. "What happened and what rig was it?" asked Garth.

"I am not sure. I think something struck the poor fellow on the rig," said Amanda.

"My God, thanks Amanda. I better get going to see what is going on," said Garth.

Garth picked up his pace as he headed to the elevators of the Maldere building. As he stood there waiting for the elevator to take him up to his office, sickly thoughts were circling around his head. He made it to his floor, and as he walked down the hallway, he could hear voices coming from Dave's office. The one voice he heard was a woman, and he picked it out right away as the voice of Ellen Sheard. The other voice he did not recognize until he could see into the office. It was Duncan Bennett, the Drilling Coordinator for Maldere. Duncan was in his thirties, had a large frame, and cast a foreboding presence wherever he went. Garth had always gotten along well with Duncan though, so he felt comfortable when he entered Dave's office.

"Excuse me. Sorry to interrupt, but what do we know of the accident? Were there other injuries? What rig was it?" asked Garth.

"Hi Garth. I was just giving Dave and Ellen an update. We have had a fatality on Executrix 30. It appears they were tripping pipe out of the hole after hitting TD. They were making a disconnection, when a bolt holding the snub line for the tongs gave way. The tongs then came forward and hit the fellow into the drawworks. He struck his head and was probably killed instantly. We have shut down all operations at the site and have called in the RCMP and Alberta Occupation Health and Safety. OHS will do their investigation of the rig and site. From all accounts, it appears the rig was using only one tong when they should have been using two to break apart the pipe," explained Duncan.

"Why would they have only used one?" asked Garth.

"I am guessing to save time, but obviously that didn't work out," said Duncan.

"Even when we get the green light to proceed drilling with Executrix, I recommend we cut them loose. Our targets will take a hit, but we will try to get another rig as soon as we can," said Duncan.

Before Dave or Ellen could say anything, Garth blurted out, "That's fine, as I think we need to rethink our strategy for this program." Ellen and Dave both shot quick, sour glances at Garth.

This did not go unnoticed by Duncan and he said, "I was hoping someone would say that. Because if we keep at this pace, we are setting ourselves up for another accident."

Finally, Dave spoke up. "Garth, we will talk about this offline. In the meantime, Duncan, send me a written report as we will need to do a press release about this."

Duncan nodded his head. "Will do. Also, we should try to reach out to the young man's family and give our condolences, and I think we should send some representatives to his funeral."

Dave replied, "Sure, we will get someone on it. Right now, it is important for us to advise Roger on the situation." Duncan shot a sideways glance at Garth and rolled his eyes as he turned around and walked out the door.

"Garth, believe me, we all feel terrible about what happened here. We will look into this and make sure it does not happen again. Having said that, we still have a huge project in front of us that we must execute. We may lose this rig, but the others will have to step it up. Like I said before, the project will go on as promised. Tyler is supposed to be back to work tomorrow. I want you to work with him on putting a revised plan together," said Dave.

Garth frowned, and he could feel his face getting redder by the second. He felt like he was finally going to blow his lid. How could this son of a bitch be so insensitive? Garth sighed and without saying a word, he turned and headed out the door and continued to his office.

Garth sat down at his desk. He looked over the map of the Copper Canyon project. The well that Executrix 30 had been drilling was one of the most southern wells. The offsetting wells in this area had proven to have little gas and lots of water. His eyes were starting to water. *Shit*, he thought. *This is definitely one well that should have never been drilled. It had no chance of being economic. I should have tried harder to stop them from drilling these wells. I swear from now on though that I am going to fight this harder; the bleeding has to stop.* Garth then picked up the phone. It was time to discuss this with Terry.

Terry was busy for most of the day, so they scheduled to meet the next morning at the usual Tim Hortons. In the afternoon, once the stock market in Toronto was closed, Maldere sent out a press release on the accident. Garth was sitting at his computer when the e-mail came through. In part, it read:

"Maldere Energy reports that yesterday, at approximately 3:30 a.m., there was a drilling rig accident at one of its sites in the Copper Canyon field. The rig was owned by Executrix and had

been contracted by Maldere. The drilling rig accident resulted in a fatality, and there were no other injuries reported.

"We are deeply saddened by this tragic loss. The safety and wellbeing of our staff and contractors is of the utmost concern to Maldere Energy. Our thoughts and prayers are with the deceased worker and his family. Maldere Energy and Executrix are working closely with Alberta Occupational Health and Safety to gather information and learn from this horrible event," said Roger Maldere, CEO at Maldere Energy.

The Copper Canyon field is a world-class natural gas deposit that is located approximately two hundred and fifty kilometres southeast of the city of Calgary. The rig in question will be shut down for the investigation, but four other rigs are still drilling, and Maldere is on schedule to be producing sixty million cubic feet per day of gas from Copper Canyon by the end of the year."

After Garth had read the release, he shook his head. *They just had to put a plug in there for the promised production. What a crock,* he thought. With that, he got up out of his chair. He didn't feel like working anymore and decided he would drink this one out instead.

That afternoon, Michelle came through the door at Garth's place. She took off her shoes and called out to Garth, but there was no reply. She looked down at the floor and knew he must be there as his shoes were sitting there. She walked around the place and then noticed Garth sitting on the patio. She came out onto the patio where Garth was sitting with a huge pile of empty beer bottles in front of him. "Rough day today?" she asked.

"There was a fatality on one of the drilling rigs," said Garth.

"Oh no! What happened?" asked Michelle.

"I am not entirely sure, but it sounds like he was struck by the pipe tongs or something," he said.

"What's worse is, do you remember me telling you about the fellow who drove me around when I was out in the field last time?" he asked. Michelle had a concerned look on her face and nodded. "Well, the poor guy who died was his nephew," he continued.

Michelle leaned forward and wrapped Garth in a hug. Garth couldn't control himself any longer, and he burst into tears. "I could have stopped it. They should have never been drilling this well. I should have halted the drilling program, at least in this area," he cried.

Michelle continued to hold him tight and said, "How? Your management wouldn't listen to you before, so how were you going to stop it?" She pulled back from Garth and considered his wet, bloodshot eyes. "This accident could have happened anywhere. You can't blame yourself for this; you weren't on the rig," she said.

"No, but I could have tried harder. I had given up," he said.

"They gave you no choice; you were placed in a no-win situation. But blaming yourself for what happened on that rig is nonsense. The accident could have happened on any well. It is not your fault," she said.

Garth said nothing but looked profoundly into her brown eyes. He loved her dearly, and he knew she was right. She was always right. "I love you," he said, and he grasped the sides of her head with both hands and gave her a long deep kiss.

"I love you too," she said. "Now let's go get some food into you. I think you have had enough beer tonight." Garth smiled and leaned his head on hers. *What would I do without her?* he thought.

The next day found Garth at the entrance of Tyler's office. Garth knocked on the door and then entered. Tyler was sitting there, looking at all of the papers on his desk. Tyler looked at Garth and smiled, "Gibbs. Good to see ya."

Garth thought to himself, *I wonder what happened to him always calling me 'Gibbins'?* However, he was pleased with the difference. Tyler's face still showed some bruising, but the swelling had gone down. Tyler's hair was actually combed and not the usual "finger in the light socket" style. Garth thought he looked pretty good after all he had been through.

"How are you doing?" asked Garth.

"Well, all things considered, I feel good. I can't sit or stand for very long, as I still get headaches, and I am sensitive to light. But all in all, for being almost dead, I think I am doing well. I am still the young stud I always was," said Tyler.

"I see you haven't lost any self-admiration through the process," Garth grinned.

"I want to thank you again, Garth – you and Michelle – for everything you did," said Tyler.

"Anyone would have done it. It just so happened we were walking by," said Garth.

"Not everyone would have done it, and believe me, I am grateful," said Tyler.

"I know you and I have butted heads a lot, but I wanted you to know that I always respected you and admired your work. Your work always made me try to work harder and be a better engineer," continued Tyler.

Garth was caught off guard by Tyler's comments. *Wow, that knock on the head has made him loopy,* he thought. Garth gulped down a huge pile of pride and said, "Thank you, Tyler. You know I have always felt the same about you. The planning and procedures you put into place on this drilling program were top notch."

Tyler smiled, "Well, the planning may have been good, but it doesn't matter how well you plan if the project isn't worth doing in the first place."

Tyler got a serious look on his face and he looked directly at Garth. The way that Tyler was concentrating on him made him uncomfortable. "Do you need a coffee? I know I could sure use one. Although I will have to get a decaf now," said Tyler. He continued, "I need to talk to you in confidence about some issues I am aware of here. These walls have ears, so let's go somewhere we can talk in private."

Garth's wheels were turning. What could it be that Tyler wanted to talk about? Garth was curious to find out. Even though he had just finished a coffee, he quickly said, "Sure I know of a place. Follow me." The two rose to their feet and vacated the office building as quickly as possible. Garth was sure if any people saw them leaving together, they wouldn't believe what they were seeing.

Garth led Tyler to the Tim Hortons that Terry and he would go to when they did not want to be seen or heard. Garth was surprised that Tyler took his coffee exactly the same way that he did, except of course, because his brain was still recovering, Tyler's was decaffeinated. They took a seat towards the back and pulled back the plastic tabs on their coffees. Tyler took a sip of the hot coffee and said, "I have not told anyone this. After my accident, it has really made me think and put things into perspective." Garth was all ears as he pondered what secrets that Tyler was going to reveal. Tyler continued, "I am not sure how to say this, but here it goes. I have been romantically involved with Ellen Sheard." Garth did not have to act to be surprised. He was not surprised by the fact, because he already knew. However, he was shocked that Tyler would actually tell him. "Holy shit, man!" said Garth with a look of incredulity.

Tyler gave a nervous look around the coffee shop before he continued. "It just kind of happened. After we had been working late on the Bear Creek acquisition, we decided to go for some beers. Well, I had a couple too many, and she gave me a ride back to my place. She came in, and we had a few more beers, and I convinced her to crash at my place and go home in the morning. We went to bed, her in my bed, and me on the couch. After about an hour, I was awoken by her removing my underwear. Well, let's just say I answered the bell." Tyler paused for a minute, thinking how he was going to tell the story without going into more detail than he wanted to.

Garth tried his best to concentrate and listen to what Tyler was saying, but he was finding it tough to get that thought of Tyler and Ellen out of his head. The thought of Tyler with anyone made him nauseous. "Anyways, afterwards, we would make plans to meet up almost every day. It went on for a couple of months, until Roger Maldere found out. You see, Roger and Ellen had been having an affair for years until she ended it last year. He threatened to fire her, but she said if he did that, she would tell his wife everything," said Tyler.

Garth listened intently. *This is getting weirder by the minute. Truth is certainly stranger than fiction,* he thought.

"So, when he found out about me and Ellen, he turned it around on her. Now he has one on her, and he is trying to force her to resign," said Tyler. Tyler again glanced around the floor to make sure no one was leaning in to eavesdrop on their conversation. "I believe you know the company Nigel West?" continued Tyler.

Garth nodded that he had and said, "They were the consultants that Dave was pushing on me to use when doing the initial evaluation of the Copper Canyon land sale."

"Right. Well, you probably don't know this, but they were used on the Bear Creek acquisition as well. It was their simulation software that was used to give the estimates of gas in place and to identify the drilling locations," said Tyler.

Garth crinkled his forehead. "I thought that Maldere said they would not be using their stuff after the work I did last year," said Garth. "I showed that there were too many flaws in the reservoir inputs they were using. Not to mention that they needed to do some serious quality control on the data they were using."

Tyler shrugged his shoulders and continued. "Well, when Sentinel would not give us the reserves we needed, we switched to Cody and Montross. Cody and Montross ate up everything that Nigel West presented, and that is how we got the favourable evaluation." Garth sat back in his chair, folded his arms, and said, "So that was Roger's doing, and you have e-mails that back this up?"

Tyler nodded his head. "I have a floppy disk that contains e-mails between the evaluation companies and Nigel West about how Roger Maldere manipulated them to get what he wanted. But that is not everything. You see, it just so happens that Roger Maldere's wife was one of the largest shareholders in Bear Creek. Roger had a shell company set up in her name that invested heavily in Bear Creek. They made a significant penny when Bear Creek was acquired. Also, since it is in his wife's name, he feared that he would lose access to the money if his wife found out about him and Ellen," said Tyler.

Garth knew that there had to be something fishy going on, but he had never expected anything like that. "And there are e-mails that confirm this?" asked Garth suspiciously.

Tyler took another quick glance around the room before he nodded his head.

"How did Ellen get these e-mails?" asked Garth.

"As VP, she was included on the e-mails with the reserve evaluators. For the others, she would not reveal the sources. What I will say though, is be careful what you send on company e-mails as you may think they are private, but they are not," said Tyler.

Garth had been cautioned on using company e-mail by others before. They said that e-mails were monitored all the time. Garth had always thought it was an office myth. Garth's mind was slowly processing all of this information, but there was one thing that he could not get his mind around. "Why did Ellen give you these e-mails?" asked Garth.

"She told me that if she was ever walked out of the office that these e-mails should make it to the media," said Tyler.

The next question then flashed in his mind, and he said, "Why are you telling me all of this?"

Tyler took a long a pause and stared into Garth's eyes. He moved his mouth as if he was going to speak then stopped to pause again. Finally, he spoke and said, "I thought you should know that, because before you start rocking the boat on this Bear Creek thing, you need to know there a lot of players who have a lot to lose and will fight to keep what they have." Tyler paused again. He looked at Garth and then looked down at his coffee. Tyler let out a sigh and said, "Also you should know that Terry Cooper is wrapped up in this Bear Creek thing. I know you see him as a mentor, but believe me, he is not to be trusted."

Garth's mouth dropped, and he shook his head and said, "I don't believe you. Terry has been a great help on this. There is no way that he is involved."

Tyler tilted his head to one side and glared back at Garth, "Really? Has he taken any of your concerns to anyone or has he just sat on them? I have heard that he is secretly trying to see you are let go."

Garth's head was reeling. "Just be careful what you divulge to Terry in the future as he may try to use it against you," said Tyler.

Garth had lost his taste for his coffee, and he pushed it away. He needed time to let what Tyler had said to him sink in. Could it be the man he trusted was really out to get him and to keep things covered up? "Thanks, Tyler," said Garth hesitantly.

"No problem. I figured it is the least I could do for the guy that saved my life," replied Tyler. Garth gave an uneasy grin as he rose from his seat and tossed his half-finished coffee in the garbage. He had the feeling that part of his soul had just been ripped out of his body.

Garth struggled to stay focused on his job for the rest of the day. He could not stop thinking about what Tyler had relayed to him today. It seemed like forever when he was finally able to step through the door of his place. He removed his shoes and immediately walked over to the refrigerator and grabbed a long-necked bottle of beer. He tipped the bottom skyward and guzzled about half of it. He watched as the foam built up inside the bottle as he brought it down and rested it on the table. He had figured there were rash and incompetent people at his work. The thought of a bigger conspiracy with so many moving parts had never crossed his mind. *What am I going to do?* he thought.

He was into his third beer when the lock turned in the door and in stepped Michelle. She saw Garth sitting at the table with one beer in his hand and two empties on the table in front of him. "I take it you had another stellar day?" she said.

"You better grab one for yourself. I have a real humdinger to tell you," said Garth. Michelle went to the fridge for a beer and sat next to Garth. She twisted off the cap and took a small swig. She held his hand and said, "What happened that has got you this worked up?"

Garth explained what Tyler had told him. Michelle sat there and quietly drank her beer as the story unfolded before her. When Garth was finished, she said, "And you believe everything that Tyler is telling you?"

Garth slowly nodded his head and shrugged his shoulders. "That is not a convincing response," she said.

"Remember, this is the guy you said was your nemesis. He is saying these things about a person who you look up to and has stood by you when others didn't. It just doesn't sound right to me," she continued.

"Well, it kind of makes sense. Terry knew about the well performance, and he never took the issue higher or tried really hard to stop it. He is the Chief Reservoir Engineer. Surely there is no way that he didn't know that Nigel West was involved," replied Garth.

Michelle continued to hold his hand and studied his brown bloodshot eyes and said, "I am sure that Terry has his reasons. Besides, he told you he was not involved in the Bear Creek acquisition. Acquisitions are usually kept pretty hush-hush in any company, and it is plausible that he never knew about their involvement. Also if Ellen and Roger knew, he would oppose. That was all the more reason to not involve him."

Garth nodded his head. It was hard to argue that.

"I have a friend at an investment firm that used to work with some of these guys," said Michelle. "We had an evening business class together at SAIT a few years ago. He always said if you want to find out what is really going on in business, follow the money to see who is the beneficiary. Let me talk to him and see what he can dig up. Let's try to find as many facts for ourselves before you act on any of this information. In the meantime, do not bring this up with Terry. If you are wrong, you will have alienated an ally, and from what I understand, you don't have many at Maldere." She had a grave look of concern on her face.

"What if I am right?" asked Garth.

"We will cross that bridge if we get there. There is more downside if you make a move on false information," said Michelle.

"I thought you really believed in Tyler," said Garth.

"He may seem different after his accident. However, I still think it is hard to change or cover up your inner self for long. Fundamentally, you are still the same deep down and nothing can really change that," said Michelle. "Now come on. I don't feel like cooking anything, and since I see that you have not begun to cook anything, we should go out for a bite somewhere, and you can tell me again why you suddenly believe Tyler."

Garth got up with her. *Boy, she sure knew how to handle him,* he thought.

The next morning found Garth in his office. He was taking turns staring at the painting outside his wall and turning the owl pendant in his hand. He was unsure what he was going to do about Terry. Should he confront him or just go on pretending that he had not heard what he had heard from Tyler? Garth did not want to offend the true friend and mentor that he had in Terry. They were scheduled to meet at 10:00 a.m. at their usual spot, and it was now 9:30. Garth had not been able to accomplish a single thing this morning. Finally at 9:45, Garth sat up and gave a long sigh. He knew what he had to do and headed out the door.

He arrived at the Tim Hortons with about five minutes to spare before 10 a.m. Garth took his position in the line up to order. There were six people ahead of him, and only one till was open. That was unusual as normally there were three tills open, and they could whisk through the orders quickly. Garth looked at the staff that was there and did not see the main server named Raul. Raul was extremely efficient at his job, and Garth marvelled at how he could remember people's orders. If a customer had been there a few times before, they did not have to say anything, as Raul knew exactly what they were going to order. He would say, "Large double, double" or "medium single, single" or " large, one milk" for people's orders, and Garth had never seen him get it wrong – although, Ken would get pleasure in trying to trick him up whenever Garth and Ken came to this location. Raul could serve three to four customers before the other servers could get through one. Without Raul there this morning, the line was moving slowly. Garth hoped that meant that Tim Hortons was giving him an all-paid vacation, because if anyone deserved something like that, it was Raul.

After about ten minutes, it was Garth's turn to order. He glanced over his shoulder and saw Terry coming through the door. Terry motioned to the table in the back that he was going to take a seat there, and Garth nodded his acceptance. Garth picked up the coffees and headed to where Terry was seated. Garth thought that Terry looked to be out of breath as though he had run here. When Garth sat down, he looked across at Terry. He appeared to be distressed as if he had just received some bad news.

Terry was fidgeting in his seat and something was obviously bothering him. "Sorry, I am late," said Terry.

"It's okay. I was in the line-up for ten minutes anyway," replied Garth.

Terry was having a hard time looking Garth in the eye and nervously played with the plastic lid on his coffee. "I just took a royal ass chewing from Roger," said Terry. Garth gave a quizzical look at Terry. Terry continued to look down and play with his coffee. Terry continued, "Apparently he took a call this morning from Craig Mills at the *Calgary Herald*. Mills was asking questions about the Copper Canyon project as he had heard that the wells were not meeting expectations. He also indicated that Maldere was going to miss their production targets for year-end by thirty million cubic per day. Then he started asking questions about the rig accident and if Maldere's practice of offering bonuses to drilling companies for quick turnarounds on drilling wells was a contributing factor." Terry then let out a huge sigh and took a sip of his coffee.

Garth continued to stare at Terry, studying his face and trying to interpret his facial expressions. "Why would he be chewing you out on that? Did he think you were the one who tipped off Mills?" asked Garth.

When Garth spoke this time, Terry picked his head up and concentrated on Garth. "Actually, he thinks it was you," said Terry.

Garth was shocked and sat back in his seat. "Me?" asked Garth.

Terry nodded his head, "Yeah. Apparently Mills did say his source was a young engineer from Maldere who had leaked the information," said Terry.

Garth was getting angry now, and he could feel the blood flushing in his cheeks. "So Maldere just assumed it was me," said Garth.

Terry never took his eyes off Garth and said, "He figures it is your way of getting your point across and stopping the Copper Canyon project. He knows you have never been a fan of it."

Garth considered this for a moment and thought, *Well, that is not really a shocker. Everyone around me would know that.*

"I told him I would talk to you to find out. It wasn't you, was it?" asked Terry.

A part of Garth felt deeply hurt that Terry would even ask him that. "No. I most certainly didn't," said Garth. He was getting defensive now and was agitated. "Let me go talk to Maldere. I want to tell him I don't appreciate the accusation," said Garth emphatically.

Terry held up his hands towards Garth, motioning him to stop. "Just wait a minute and hear me out," said Terry.

"I know you want to go in there and set him straight, but that would be a mistake. Our next move has to be calculated carefully. He will just shut down anything you say, and all you will get out of it is some walking paper," said Terry.

"That's fine. I don't want to work for an asshole like him anyhow," said Garth.

Terry furrowed his forehead deeply and said, "Look, remember the oil patch in Calgary is like a small town where everyone knows your business. You do not want to get canned by a guy like Maldere, as it can cripple your career. If it gets known around town to the wrong people in high places here, you will be grounded before you even get started."

Garth knew Terry was right, and he settled back into his chair. He was getting so mad that he could feel tears in the corner of his eyes. Garth didn't know why, but whenever he got real mad, it would bring his eyes to water, and they were sure watering now.

Terry took a deep breath and continued. "Numbers and calculations come easy to you and me. We can figure things out that nobody else can, and that is what makes us good engineers. If we did not have to deal with people, the job would be easy; however, if you want to be a great engineer, you have to master how to work with people. That is where so many engineers fall apart, as they can't. You may be the smartest guy in the room, but if you can't get people to buy in and support your ideas, you may as well have a broom in your hand.

"Now Maldere was talking to me on how he was going to rebut Mill's questions. He has been coached on this matter by your old friends at Nigel West. His response is going to be that people are using conventional engineering concepts on this play, but it is an unconventional resource that requires unconventional thinking. On the issue of the water, Nigel West is comparing it to coal bed methane where the reservoir has to be depressurized to release the gas that is adsorbed into the coal, or in this case, the shale. By producing the water, the water pressure will be reduced, allowing gas to break out and be produced," said Terry. Garth had heard of this before, but also heard that operators had to produce some of these wells for over a year for the gas to flow up the well to surface. Terry continued. "Now I am not sure if that is possible here, but this explanation is enough to confuse the media. At the same time, it will satisfy the masses to buy some time for Maldere before being placed in the penalty box by the market."

"This is not the first time I have heard people throw out the unconventional card as being an explanation for why wells don't perform as expected. It is being used as a way to explain large gas in place and unexpected well results. If the well is not performing, they say, "Well, it is unconventional," so it will decline to a certain rate and then it will flatten out and produce for seemingly forever. You just have to believe. I am worried about the industry going forward as people have stopped thinking and are placing blind faith in the unconventional religion and Nigel West is leading the charge. We are now pulling reservoir engineers out of hard hats everywhere and are losing the art of truly evaluating reservoirs. We have type curves everywhere in corporate presentations. 'Production is exceeding the type curve,' they say all the time. Great, but what the hell is the type curve based on? Certainly not actual reservoir parameters." Terry then took a pause, gave a sideways grin, and then continued. "Well, that is enough of my bitch session. Sorry I kind of went off on a tangent. It is something I do when under pressure."

"I still think I should set him straight. I was looking for a job when I found this one, and I would be free of all of those idiots," said Garth defiantly.

Terry shook his head and said, "I know that you think that going to another company will solve all of your problems. Listen to me though. If you think you will get away from the Rogers, Daves, and Tylers of the industry, you are sadly mistaken. There are those types of people at every company. They will have different names, but believe me, they are everywhere you go, and you have to learn how to cope with these people, or you are going to bang your head and be frustrated wherever you go."

Garth let Terry's last statement sink in. He knew Terry was right. Running away might make him feel better for the short term, but it was not a permanent solution. Garth watched Terry take a sip of his coffee. He seemed to have settled himself down by getting this off of his chest. Garth could tell Terry was just as frustrated as he was. Garth just had to ask him a question to put his mind at ease. "Did you know that Nigel West worked on the Bear Creek acquisition?" Garth asked.

Terry looked up from his coffee. Garth watched as Terry's face turned from one of content to the face of a fearful child when his father had discovered some bad thing the child had done. Terry's eyes never strayed as he said, "I knew that Nigel West was working with our guys on something. But I swear I did not know it was this acquisition. Who told you that they worked on it?"

Garth studied Terry's face for hints that he wasn't telling the truth, but Terry's facial expressions seemed to be sincere. "Tyler," replied Garth.

"Tyler is your trusted friend now?" said Terry with an air that sounded patronizing to Garth.

"Keep your enemies close, right?" replied Garth.

Terry looked on with a blank stare before he spoke. "Well, he should know. Hmm, that explains a lot actually," said Terry. "I should have known from the presentation our guys gave that it was influenced by Nigel West."

"How could you have not known?" asked Garth.

"Believe it or not, I am not held within their confidence. They do not include me on things they think I will disagree on," said Terry.

"But you are the Chief Reservoir Engineer," said Garth.

"That is only a title. They only include me when it is convenient or when I have rocked the boat hard enough," said Terry.

Garth couldn't help to feel skeptical, but at the same time, Terry had always appeared supportive to Garth.

Terry looked down at his wristwatch and exclaimed, "Sorry Garth, but I have to get back to the office."

Garth was disappointed. He had more questions he wanted to ask, but they would have to wait.

Terry rose up from the table and said, "Thanks for the coffee. Garth, please don't do anything rash. We will get this figured out eventually."

Garth remained seated and looked up at Terry. "You bet. Take care, Terry," he replied. Garth watched Terry walk out of the store and head down the sidewalk in the direction of the Maldere building. Terry had said all of the right things, but Garth still had an uneasy feeling that Terry wasn't telling him everything.

Garth got up out of his chair and tossed his empty coffee cup into the waste receptacle. He walked out onto the sidewalk and looked up into the sun. It felt warm on his face, which was in contrast to the chill that was in the air. *Winter is right around the corner,* he thought. Garth thought about heading back to work, but something in him made him want to go for a stroll and soothe his thoughts before heading back. He walked down the sidewalk towards where Michelle worked. Maybe he could get her and go for an early lunch.

He was only a block away from her office tower when he passed a small trendy coffee shop. It was a type of establishment that Garth would not normally set foot in. For one, his unpolished, country-hick background stood out from the other prim urban coffee drinkers. This made him extremely uncomfortable, as he knew as well as the other patrons that he did not belong there. Secondly, he hated having to spend two minutes trying to order a five-dollar coffee that tasted like the coffee that his Grandpa used to make with six scoops of Nabob in a drip machine. Normally he would not even glance at a place like this, but something or someone caught his eye.

He slowed his pace as he looked at the beautiful, flowing red hair of a girl who had her back to him. She was sitting across from a well-dressed man with a clean-shaven face and streaked blond hair. The immaculate hair looked as if it had been blow-dried and would crack under pressure if someone were foolish enough to touch it. Garth smirked, *Now that is the type of guy I would expect at an establishment such as this,* he thought. As he continued to walk past, the man then leaned forward and gave the woman a kiss. As she turned her head to greet his lips with her cheek, Garth's fears were realized; it was Michelle. Garth quickly turned his eyes away and started to walk in the opposite direction.

Garth felt rage building up from within. *I knew it was too good to be true with her,* he thought. Every woman he had ever gotten close to seemed to find a way to tear out his heart and leave him standing by the boulevard, wondering what went wrong. Tears were streaming down Garth's face when he made it back to the office tower. He wiped them away and turned his head to the side when he met anyone.

When Garth got back to his office, he quickly ducked inside and shut the door. He had managed to make it back without anyone really noticing him. He looked down at his chair, and there was a green card that was five by seven inches with a red stamp on it sitting on the seat. Garth recognized it immediately as a High Five card. The High Five card was a motivational program that Maldere was using for one employee to recognize another employee for a job well done. Once an employee accumulated five of them, they could trade them in for $100 on their next pay stub. It was a program that Garth found amusing, as many corporations were using something similar. Garth had joked that some HR people had gone to the same conference and came back to their respective companies and implemented the same recognition program.

He picked up the card and saw there was a three-and-a-half-inch floppy disk below it. He read the card and saw that it was from Tyler. The card read: *"Gibbs, this card is in recognition of the great work you have done on the Copper Canyon project. I know it has been a difficult task for you, but I wanted to let you know I think your work is first class. Maldere should be proud to have you on its team."*

Garth read the card over three times before his mind actually comprehended the words as his mind was still off thinking about Michelle.

Garth gave out a scornful snort when he read the card. *I bet Maldere is proud all right*, he thought. He then turned the floppy disk over in his hand, studying it. There was nothing written on the adhesive label that would indicate what information the disk contained. Absent-mindedly, Garth placed the disk into his computer's drive and listened to the grinding noises as the metal hub of the disk mated with the spindle of the computer's drive. Finally the disk appeared in the file explorer, and Garth noticed there was only one folder on the disk. The folder was nameless, and Garth clicked on the icon, and it opened to reveal ten files.

Garth opened the files one by one. They were all scanned images of e-mails that belonged to Roger Maldere. The e-mails were just like Tyler had described, as they were a smoking gun revealing how Maldere had manipulated the reserve evaluators. The most surprising e-mail to Garth was the one between Maldere and his broker with regards to Bear Creek. Garth was not only astounded by the e-mail that left no doubt as to the business conflict, but how the hell did Ellen and Tyler ever get a hold of this? Garth had a fluttering feeling in his chest just like he was standing on the edge of a high cliff.

Garth closed the files and ejected the disk from his computer. He seized the disk and sprinted out of his office and headed for Tyler's office. He rushed so fast out of his office that he had not bothered to look both ways before entering the hallway. He nearly knocked over Lindsey, one of the production technicians. He said "sorry" and continued towards his destination as Lindsey looked on with a bemused face. He could see that Tyler was not in his office as the motion detection light was off. He stood at the doorway and looked around.

Tyler's desk was cleaner than he had ever seen it. There were no loose papers, pens, or old food wrappers in sight.

As he stood there probing the office with his eyes, thinking about where Tyler could be, he smelled a sickening sour smell. He did not need to look around, as he knew that Peter Bozak was behind him. Garth slowly turned his head and Peter said, "Tyler is not in."

Garth raised his eyebrows and thought, *No shit, Sherlock,* but instead, Garth said, "Do you know where he is?"

Peter studied Garth for a moment and said, "I guess you haven't heard, but he was having setbacks with his recovery, so they gave him a couple of weeks off. I believe he went to his grandparents in the Okanagan to decompress."

Peter had a weird smirk on his face that annoyed Garth as if he knew more but was not going to divulge more information to him. Garth said thanks to Peter and headed back to his office.

Before he got to his office, he could hear his phone ringing. He rounded the corner and raced over to the phone. He looked at the display: It was Michelle. Garth's heart raced. He reached out to pick up the handset but stopped himself. He had no clue what he was going to say to her, and he didn't feel like confronting her right now. The phone continued to ring and eventually went to his voice mail. After about thirty seconds, the red light on the side of the phone came on indicating she had left him a message. He stared at the phone for a moment, and then with a sigh, he got up from his desk to leave.

Garth had his head down and did not see Roger Maldere standing in his doorway. Garth looked up at the last minute; otherwise, he might have run into him. Seeing Roger Maldere there startled Garth, and his face went white.

"Garth, I would like to have a word with you," said Roger. Roger's tone was gruff and edgy, so Garth knew this was not going to be a social call.

"Sure," said Garth as he turned and melded back into his chair. Maldere entered the office and closed the door behind him. Garth looked down nervously at the disk that lay on his desk. Roger's eyes followed Garth's gaze down to the little black piece of plastic. His eyes stared there for a moment then turned back to Garth's where they burned into them.

"I want to talk to you about the Copper Canyon project," said Roger. From his voice, Garth could tell he was trying to hide his anger and frustration. There was the slightest quiver in his voice that gave it a way.

"Sure," said Garth. Garth knew that his eyes were red from crying, and Roger seemed to be evaluating his face for signs of why.

"I took a call from the asshole Craig Mills at the *Calgary Herald* this morning," seethed Roger. Garth thought calling Craig Mills an asshole was consistent for Maldere. During the second quarter results conference call, Maldere had been recorded calling Mills an asshole under his breath when he had asked a question about Maldere's debt. He had thought he said it quietly enough, but the microphones had picked it up clearly.

Maldere's eyes narrowed as he continued. "It appears someone from this company has been telling him confidential information about some unexpected well results and that we are going to fall well short of our production targets this year. He is recommending to people to short our stock. I now have to waste my time and put a statement together explaining to this brain-dead asshole and others like him that this is an unconventional play, and it requires an untraditional method of evaluation. The old rules of thumb for conventional reservoirs do not apply when it comes to unconventional plays such as what we have in Copper Canyon." When Roger had finished, he paused and studied Garth's face again for signs that would prove to him that Garth was the one that had leaked the information.

"It looks like you have been crying. It wouldn't be that you regret having given this information to Mills, would it?" Roger said with a smile.

Before Garth had collected his thoughts, he responded, "If you think it was me who informed Mills, you are greatly mistaken. I have concerns about the well performance; that is no mystery. I am also skeptical about the "unconventional" explanation, but I did not give any information to Mills. In fact, I resent being blamed for this."

Roger sat back in his chair and folded his arms, never letting his eyes stray from Garth's face. "I know that you have been working with Terry about this program. I think you should know that today is Terry's last day at Maldere. He is going to step down and take early retirement at my request."

A look of fear and uncertainty come over Garth's face. Garth could tell that this was noticed by Roger's smug look. "When I find out that you released the information, I will send you out on your ass so quick it will make your head spin." Roger's face was turning red, and he was seething. Through gritted teeth, Roger continued. "Young punks like you, who think they know everything right out of school, make me sick. You want the big man's chair before you have ever accomplished anything and think it should just be handed to you. I have been doing this for too long and worked too hard to have some goddam little prick, stubble jumper come in here and mess it up."

Garth was getting extremely mad now. Roger was pushing all of his buttons, but Garth was unable to respond to this latest barrage. He never had hated Roger Maldere before, but now he was revealing his true character when he was faced with some controversy. In that moment, Garth realized there wasn't much that he liked about Roger Maldere. Garth let Maldere finish his beratement, and when he was finished, he simply responded, "Like I said, I had nothing to do with the information breach. With all due respect, the last thing I want is *your* chair. So, if you have no further words of encouragement, I should get back to work."

Roger raised an eyebrow and sucked on his teeth. "Very well," said Roger, "but it seems to me you are running out of support for these games you are playing. I have never understood why an employee would try to sabotage the company that puts food on their table."

Garth did not hesitate with his reply. "I know you don't understand, but I am actually trying to save this company from imploding. The right thing here is to stop doing the wrong thing." Roger rolled his eyes and walked out.

As soon as Roger had left, Garth picked up the phone and rang Terry's desk. He needed to get Terry's side of the story and ask him questions that he was unable to at coffee. The phone rang and rang and went to voice mail. Terry was either not there, or he wasn't answering. Garth left a voice mail asking Terry to call him as soon as possible. Garth placed the handset back into its cradle and looked down at the red light that was still flashing, reminding him of the message from Michelle. He rose up from his desk and gave a look around. His eyes caught the little black disk sitting there by his computer monitor. It seemed as a beacon to him. *Well, if Roger is upset with some little well results, let's see how the son of a bitch likes this hitting the press,* he thought. He scooped up the disk and took an envelope out of his desk. He placed the disk in the envelope and ran out of the office.

After a brief detour, Garth finally made it home. He opened the door and kicked off his shoes. With all of the things going on, he had not thought of Michelle. Now that he was home, that was all he could think of. He got a beer out of the fridge and headed out onto the deck.

As he sat there with only his thoughts for company, he polished off beer after beer. Each one tasted better than the one before. He heard the front door open and knew Michelle was here. He felt a growing sickness in his stomach, as he still wasn't sure how to confront her about what he had seen at the coffee shop. She stepped out onto the deck with a beer in her hand, bent over, and gave Garth a kiss before she took her place in a chair beside him. "Another day in paradise?" she asked.

"You know it. Today was a doozy, putting all others before it to shame," he replied.

"Well, I have some interesting news for you. I met with my friend from the investment firm," said Michelle.

"Oh, and what's his name?" asked Garth with an air of contentiousness.

She gave a puzzled look and said, "Nick Grubman."

Garth was vibrating in all of his extremities, and he felt like he would explode.

"What's going on?" she asked.

Garth gave a wry, drunken smile and leaned into her and said, "I saw you today sucking face with good ole Mr. Grubman. Looked like quite the business meeting."

Michelle's face showed a momentary expression of shock, but then she gathered herself and sternly said, "I don't know what you think you saw, but we certainly weren't 'sucking face' as you call it."

Garth turned his head, gave a sarcastic sneer, and said, "I know what I saw."

Michelle shook his arm and got his attention before she continued. "No, I don't think you do. Nick and I were boyfriend and girlfriend at one time, yes. Maybe I should have told you, but I didn't think it was necessary as it was in the past. He had only gave me a kiss on the cheek, which I told him was not appropriate, and I certainly did not reciprocate. I love you, you dumb bastard."

Garth pulled back his arm and said, "Well, you have a shitty way of showing it."

"I was getting information for you," Michelle interjected. "I told you. You need to follow the money to see who the big benefiter is before you do anything."

Again, Garth gave a sarcastic sigh and said, "It's too late for that. I have set the plans for the future for Maldere already, and it doesn't include that son of a bitch. He thought he could bully me, but tomorrow we will find out what he is made of when it hits the press." He smiled and leaned back in his chair waiting for Michelle's response.

"You didn't?" she said with a huge disappointment. "You dumb ass. You know who benefits from any scandal about Roger Maldere?"

Garth, proud of himself, mockingly said, "Certainly not Roger."

Michelle shook her head and continued. "No not him, but your good buddies at Nigel West do."

Now it was Garth's turn to be confused, and his forehead furrowed as he said, "What the hell are you talking about?"

Michelle gave a sympathetic sigh. "Nick has it from a good source that Nigel West had been trying to do a big joint venture in Texas on some gas play there, but Maldere wanted nothing to do with it. Apparently, Roger did not want to venture into the United Sates."

Garth blankly stared at her and said, "Well, no matter, they still won't be getting anything."

Michelle shook her head and said, "No, it does matter. You see, if anything happens to Roger, they will promote Tim Kane."

Garth shrugged. "So, Tim will be better than the old man."

Michelle gave a sigh of exasperation and said, "Oh really? Did you know that he is good friends with the founders of Nigel West, and rumour has it that he has been receiving kick-backs from them? If he gets in control, he will do whatever Nigel West wants."

Now Garth was white, and he was trying to shake the cobwebs out of his fermented, foggy mind. "How does your boyfriend know this?"

Michelle shrugged and said, "You are my boyfriend, dummy. Nick did not reveal his sources, but he is usually right on these things."

Garth gave a sarcastic laugh. "Usually."

Michelle nodded and said, "I believe him."

"Of course you do. Why wouldn't you? You trusted him enough to sleep with him," said Garth.

"Now hold it right there. You are drunk and are crossing way over the line. Don't blame me for something you did."

"Who's blaming who? Tomorrow will be a brighter day without Maldere. And when these things don't come to fruition, you can come back and apologize."

Michelle was mad, and she tucked her hair behind her ears and crossed her arms. "Me apologize to you? I think you are sadly mistaken, Mr. Gibbins." She jumped to her feet and looked down at Garth, tears welling in her eyes. Before she walked out the door, she turned back to look at Garth and said, "Call me when you grow up." With that, she was gone with a resounding slam of the door.

Garth sat there, and he looked down at the empty bottles in front of him. *Shit, she drank my last beer,* he thought.

Garth placed his face in his hands. *Why did I say that?* he thought. *Drunk or not, there is no excuse for that. How could this get any worse? I am in a real pickle now.* Garth was rocking back and forth with his head still cradled in his hands when the phone rang. *Good, it's Michelle, and I can apologize,* he thought.

He looked at the display and saw it was his dad calling. He stared at the phone and then answered. "Hi Dad. How are things?"

"Hey, Garth," said Jack. "Things are good here. We have the canola swathed, and hopefully, we can start combining soon. It would be great if you and Michelle could come out here for a bit. Sure could use the help, and I would love to see that wonderful woman again."

The words bit into Garth. "I would love too," he said. "It is pretty crazy at work right now, so I don't know if I will be able to break away. Besides, I am not sure if Michelle will want to see me again."

"What?" asked Jack. "What happened? I thought you two were getting pretty serious." Garth sighed, "We were. But a bunch of stuff has happened at work, and we had a fight tonight."

Jack replied, "You know, Garth, a woman like that doesn't come around often. I would suggest you swallow some pride and try to make it up with her."

"You don't even know what happened and you're taking her side?" said Garth. Garth was still riding his beer buzz and knew he had responded more sternly than he would have under normal conditions.

"I am just telling you there are way more important things than work. Work will always be there, no matter how much you neglect it, but a good woman won't be."

Garth breathed into the phone, "I guess you should know." As soon as he said it, he lowered his head and thought, *Damn, I am going to alienate everyone.*

"Okay. Garth, I wanted to tell you this in person one day, but I never got up the balls. Since we are hundreds of miles away right now, I will try to explain it on the phone. If you want to know the real reason why your mom left, it is because I have suffered from depression for many years. I grew distant from your mom. I never even knew I was doing it, but she did. She mistook my depression as if I was having an affair with someone. I was always moody, and eventually I pushed her away to another man," said Jack. Garth could hear his voice cracking as he spoke.

"Why did you wait so long to tell me?" asked Garth. "I always thought it was because of me."

"I am sorry, Garth. I never sought help until after my heart attack. The weirdest thing, you know. When I thought I was dying, all I could think about is how much I wanted to live. I had contemplated killing myself for so long, and when the time had finally come, I realized it was the last thing I wanted."

Garth's mind was trying to process this overload of information. He had always looked at his dad as an impenetrable pillar and could not believe he had contemplated ending his own life.

"I needed to tell you this to get it off my chest. It had been weighing me down for far too long. Communication is the key to getting through this. Remember, I am here whenever you need help. I can't help you much with any work-related issues, as I know little about what you do. I can though give you advice on Michelle. She is a great woman, and you need to do whatever it takes to make it right with her."

Garth sighed, "I know."

They talked for close to half an hour like they were old friends. "Garth, why don't you get some rest," said Jack. "Tomorrow will be a brighter day. Call on Michelle and talk things through with her."

Garth said good-bye and hung up the phone. He sat down in front of the computer and began searching about depression. He read about the symptoms. As he read, he realized he too showed many of the signs. He wandered over many websites about the issue. As he was searching, he thought of Andy Heywood and the emotions he must be going through. Garth pulled up the website of the obituary for Darren Heywood, Andy's nephew who had been killed in the rig accident.

The obituary told of how he was only 23 years old and was survived by his mother Sharon and father Dale. It went on to tell about the things he loved: the outdoors, farming, hockey, music, and most of all, his special girlfriend. He had planned on returning to the farm but wanted to earn as much money as he could in the oilfield first to get him started. Garth read on emotionless. He read a phrase that was attached to the piece: *"Drink the water of the Peace River, and you will return."* When Garth read this, he started to sob openly as he thought of how Darren did return but in a casket. *You will not die in vain,* thought Garth.

Chapter 8

The next morning found Garth at the C-train station with the droves of people headed to work. He overheard a man talking to a woman. "Did you hear about Maldere?" asked the man.

"Sure did," she replied. "The man is a pig and deserves everything that is coming to him. He should be up on harassment charges as well."

Garth hurried over to the newspaper dispenser and picked up a copy of the *Calgary Herald.* He eyed the headline: *"Roger Maldere's Fall from Grace: Huge Scandal Brewing at Calgary Energy Company Darling"* by Craig Mills. By the time Garth arrived at the office, the place was abuzz. Conversations were going on all over the office, and everyone was talking about the newspaper headlines and how this was going to affect them going forward. Garth did not join in any of the water cooler talk and continued to his office. He sat down and booted up his computer when Tyler bolted into his office. This startled Garth, and he looked up, "Tyler, I thought you were at your grandparents for a couple of weeks?"

Tyler gave a surprised look and said, "No, I just went there for a couple of days. Who told you I was going be gone for a couple of weeks?"

"Stinky Pete," said Garth.

Tyler just shrugged and said, "That guy can never get anything right." Tyler then sat down at one of the guest chairs in front of Garth's desk. He had a satisfied and proud look on his face. "Wow, quite the happenings around here, eh?"

Tyler leaned in and rested his arms on Garth's desk. "It looks as though Craig Mills got his hands on some e-mails that I am sure Roger Maldere was hoping would never see the light of day," said Tyler. Tyler then glanced over his shoulder to make sure no one was eavesdropping on their conversation and continued, "How did you get the disk to Mills?"

Garth hesitated and surveyed Tyler for a moment and said, "I don't know what you are talking about."

Tyler smiled a wry smile and said, "Awesome. That's exactly what to say if anyone comes asking." Satisfied, Tyler got up from the chair and turned to leave, but before he walked out the door, he turned and said, "I hear the new CEO will be Tim Kane, and he will need a new Chief Reservoir Engineer." With that Tyler turned his back, and as quickly as he had entered, he was gone.

Garth sat there and stared blankly at his computer screen. He then looked at the owl pendant hanging there. It reminded him of Michelle, and it looked like this was going just like she had predicted. Or more correctly, like her ex-boyfriend had predicted. Garth thought, *Well, the battle has been engaged, and let's see how this plays out.*

As the days passed, announcements were made at Maldere. The Alberta Securities Commission released a statement that they had begun an investigation of inside trading against Roger Maldere and Maldere's CFO. In light of the investigation, Roger Maldere was forced to step down by the Board of Directors. Tim Kane was promoted to CEO, and Dave Piett had been promoted to COO to backfill the hole left by Kane's promotion. When Garth heard about Piett's promotion, his heart sank and so did any fantasies he might have had of moving up the ladder.

Garth had just returned to his desk from the morning coffee with the guys when Tyler strode into his office. Tyler was grinning from ear to ear, and he looked to Garth like he was going to explode from the information he was containing within.

"Tyler, how is it going?" asked Garth.

Tyler wanted to hide it for longer, but he could not hold it in any longer. "Pretty good Gibbs. You are looking at the new Chief Reservoir Engineer," he said.

Garth felt as if he had been hit with a two by four. Hesitantly he said, "Congrats."

Tyler continued, "I just came from a meeting with Dave and Tim. I also learned that Peter Bozak was promoted to Dave Piett's old position. So, I guess that means you will have a new boss." That two by four that had hit Garth's head now turned into a four by four.

"Peter should be a good boss for you. Better than Big Dave was anyways," said Tyler.

Garth looked at him angrily and said, "I think that stinks...literally."

Tyler gave a nervous laugh. "Well, maybe you can come work for me. It's the least I can do to pay you back. You are the one who set this whole thing in motion with the disk that Tim gave me."

Garth looked down at the floor, and at first it did not register with him what Tyler had said. When it kicked in, he looked up and glared into Tyler's eyes. "I thought you got the disk from Ellen?"

Tyler did not miss a beat, and he said, "Oh, did I say Tim? Sorry, I meant Ellen. My mind just ain't the same sometimes. Still affected from the knock to the noggin I took, I guess."

Garth gave him a sideways glance and continued. "This was all planned from the beginning, wasn't it? Kane has been fighting for Maldere's job all the time, and he saw this as a golden opportunity."

Tyler sat back in the chair and put his hands down on the armrests. Garth looked down at Tyler's hands and could see that they were turning white as they were tensing and gripping the rests too tightly.

A light bulb went on in Garth's head. "You were the one who leaked the well results, weren't you? You knew that Maldere would think it was me and come after me. That is why you gave me the disk, as you hoped I would get mad enough and leak the disk. If it backfired, it would be on me and no one would believe that you were involved."

Tyler's face beamed, and he looked to the side and then looked back directly at Garth and said, "You got me, Gibbins. It wasn't supposed to play out this way, but I see how personally you take things, and we thought we could use it to our advantage."

Garth was steaming mad, and he could feel those anger tears building up in his eyes. Garth spat, "We? You mean Kane and you?"

Tyler shrugged. "He came to me months ago with a plan to put Maldere out to pasture. The plan he hitched was a little different, but circumstances led us down a different path."

Garth seethed. "That's when you decided to play me instead."

Tyler said, "Hey, it just happened. Besides, it is all going to work out for you in the end. You should be happy."

Garth was exasperated. "Happy? How do you figure that? Innocent people lost their jobs, and people who don't deserve a job got promoted. Not to mention that people got physically hurt and one even died in all of this mess."

Tyler motioned his hands towards Garth to calm Garth down. "Now hold on there. Who is innocent, really? This is business. Everyone has skeletons in their closet. If you are referring to Terry, he was not all that innocent, believe me. Why do you think he went away so quietly? If he were so innocent, don't you think he would stick around and try to defend himself? And yes, a man lost his life. That is tragic. But here's a newsflash for you: Drilling rigs are dangerous, and people die on them all the time, and probably always will. That is why they get paid the big bucks."

Garth could feel the skin on his nose pulsing as he replied, "You heartless bastard. And you would set me up to fry. Someone who saved your worthless hide."

Now it was Tyler's turn to get mad, and he leaned into Garth's face over the desk. "Oh, you saved my life, you say. The way I hear it, Michelle is the one who saved me. You were so drunk you were pissing in your pants and sucking your thumb. You couldn't have saved a drowning man in a birdbath."

Tyler smirked. "By the way, I heard from the grapevine that Michelle is available. Maybe I should look her up, since we kind of already have this life bond."

Garth rose to his feet. "Get the fuck out of my office. If you ever go near her, I will continue what those guys in the alley started."

Tyler mockingly nodded his head. "You were always a sore loser, Gibbins. Sometimes you just make it too easy."

Garth fumed as he watched Tyler strut out of his office. He had been had. Garth stood there and waited for his blood pressure to die down, and then he made his way to the elevator. It was time to take this up with the head schemer.

Garth made his way to the elevators and pressed the up button. Two women who worked on the floor with Garth were standing by the elevators chatting. When they saw Garth, they quickly stopped their conversation and went through the side door towards their offices. Garth absently stared at the wall as he waited for the elevator to arrive. Finally, after two minutes, there was a ding to signal the arrival of the elevator. The doors opened, and Garth was surprised to see that it was empty. He entered the elevator car and pushed the button for the 28th floor.

The ride up was uninterrupted, and the elevator stopped and opened to reveal the Roman architecture of the top floor. Seated at a desk across the atrium was a pretty, young, blonde-haired lady. She looked up from her desk at this unexpected guest and gave a quizzical look as Garth approached her desk.

"Hello Cindy," Garth said as he tried to fake a smile to hide the apprehension and frustration on his face. She looked at him and rested her elbows on the desk and said, "What can I do for you?"

Garth said, "I was wondering if Tim Kane is around as I would like to take up ten minutes of his time, if I could."

Cindy looked Garth up and down and seemed to be unimpressed with how he was dressed. Showing her annoyance, she said in a sarcastic voice, "Mr. Kane is in a meeting at the moment, and his day is booked up. Would you like to leave a message for him and maybe he will contact you when he gets a chance? As you can imagine, his days are consumed with meetings right now."

Garth shook his head and gave a sigh. "Alright, you can tell him Garth Gibbins was here to see him," he said.

"And to what is it pertaining, Mr. Gibbins?" asked Cindy.

"Tell him I would like to discuss the business plan for Copper Canyon."

Cindy scratched this down on a note pad. Garth watched her write the message, as he was suspicious that it would ever get to Tim Kane. He said thank you to Cindy and walked back to the elevators. When he was ten feet from the elevators, the bell dinged, and the doors opened. Tim Kane and Dave Piett walked out of the elevators, and both were startled to see Garth standing there.

Dave Piett was the first to speak and he said, "Garth, what are you doing here?"

Garth quickly looked at Dave, and then he turned his attention to Tim Kane. "I was hoping to borrow a couple minutes of your time, Tim, if I could," said Garth.

"You should probably go through me first. We do have a chain of command around here, you know. I know how you seem to forget the company protocol," snapped Dave.

Tim Kane put a hand up in front of Dave and said, "That's okay, Dave. I always have time for our staff. Follow me, Garth. I have about ten minutes before I have to head out to another meeting."

Dave gave a loud "humph" and watched suspiciously as Garth followed Tim to Cindy's desk. "Any messages for me Cindy?" asked Tim.

She handed him a stack of sticky notes and said, "You have three. One from your wife, one from the *Calgary Herald*, and one from Nolan Ward.

Nolan Ward, thought Garth. *He is one of the principals at Nigel West.*

Tim picked up the notes and looked back at Garth. He gave an assuring smile and motioned Garth to follow him into his office. The CEO's office was massive – four times the size of a normal office. There was a huge mahogany desk at one end, and at the other was a large coffee table surrounded by a leather black couch and matching chairs. There was a huge window that looked out towards the Rocky Mountains west of the city. As Tim walked around to his desk, he motioned to one of the leather guest chairs in front of his desk, "Have a seat." Garth nervously took a seat, he could feel himself starting to sweat, and he realized he had no clue about what he was going to say.

"So, what is on your mind?" asked Tim. Garth's voice cracked as he said, "Well, first off, congrats on the new position." Tim gave an appreciative nod. "I am not sure how to begin, but I guess I wanted to know what your plans are for the Copper Canyon project," said Garth.

"Sure. Well, we plan to finish out drilling everything we have licensed, and then we will evaluate what we have before we make any decisions on its future. Of course, we are not happy with the results of the wells. It would have been good to know the wells were under performing rather than finding out through the back door with the media," said Tim coldly as he looked down at Garth.

Garth was expecting Tim to act frigidly, so he quickly responded, "Dave Piett was informed every step of the way, and he chose not to reveal any of the well details to the people above him. As much as people think I do not follow protocol, I did."

Tim did not waver and he continued. "Don't you think something that was so impactful to the future of the corporation should have been escalated up the ladder rather than given to the press to make us look like fools with our pants down?"

Garth was not amused. "Look, you can stop this charade. You know as well as I do that I did not leak the well information to the press. We both know who did and under whose direction, and you were well aware of what was going on. You then used this against Maldere to make sure he took the fall."

Tim leaned forward on his desk and rested on his elbows. Garth could see the irritation on his face. "Look, young man, I can assure you I do not know what you are talking about. Roger Maldere was a smart man, but he had been at the helm for too long. He was becoming complacent, and he was not going to be able to steer us in a new direction. Unconventional plays are going to be the future of this industry, and Roger wanted to drag his feet and was going to miss a huge opportunity."

Garth tilted his head to the side as he said, "The opportunity you are talking about... this involves Nigel West, doesn't it? Roger did not want to sign the deal with them. I am guessing because he was not going to get the financial benefit, right? And that is why you set him up, because you knew he would blindly believe bloated well information because he was so committed to the Bear Creek acquisition. He had to make it work at all costs."

"As amusing as this conversation is, it is starting to wander from reality and relevance. This ship is headed in a new direction, and you can either get on board or stay on shore. I really don't care which. So, a few wells did not work out. Thankfully, my new Chief Reservoir Engineer pointed out the problems before they got way out of control through mismanagement," sneered Tim.

Garth was starting to vibrate, and every inch of his body was tingling. "I was the one who pointed this out right from the start. This was all a bunch of bull shit."

Tim sighed, "And alas, here we sit. Again, this corporation is headed for great things, and you are welcome to come or you can feefo. It is no skin off my nose."

Garth was puzzled, "What is feefo?"

Tim smiled. "Fit in or fuck off. F-I-F-O." Tim smiled down at Garth for effect and then rose from his desk. "Young man, your ten minutes are up." Tim pointed to the door, and Garth stood and headed towards it. He could barely feel his tingling feet as he walked across the plush carpet.

Garth slowly turned and said, "What if the media was to find out about your scheme?"

Tim gave a twisted smile. "You are going to sell your story to them? The company whistleblower that engineered the demise and deception of Roger Maldere, the great founder of this company?" Tim continued, "Go ahead. But remember all of the trails lead back to you. Now I really must go. Please see yourself out."

Garth felt like he had been just punched in the gut. His head was swimming as he waited for the elevator. *I am surrounded by assholes*, he thought to himself. Finally, after what seemed like an eternity, the elevator arrived. Garth entered the car and pressed the button for the elevator to take him back to his floor. Garth had his head down, and he was not paying attention as he steamed back to his office. He entered his office and a wall of body odour overtook him. Garth gagged a bit as that sickening sour smell filled his nostrils. There was no mistaking the smell, and he knew that Stinky Pete had been in his office. Garth speculated that Pete wanted to rub it in about his promotion and that he was now Garth's boss. He looked around his office and saw that some things had been moved, as if someone was looking for something. *That bastard is always sticking his nose where it doesn't belong*, Garth thought. His mind was made up for what he needed to do next.

Garth sat down at his computer and started copying his personal files to floppy disks. As he waited for information to be downloaded, he set about tidying up all of his personal items and placing them in cardboard moving boxes he collected from the copier room. He looked down at the owl token hanging off of his screen and placed it over his neck. He was staring at the picture outside of his office when he saw a shadow move across it, and he then he saw the figure of Peter Bozak come into view.

Peter stepped into Garth's office. "Garth, you are finally here," said Peter. "You have probably heard, but I just wanted to let you know that I am going to be the new Reservoir Manager."

Garth looked up at Pete with a distinct look of annoyance on his face. "Yeah, I heard," was his gruff reply.

Peter frowned and his brow furrowed. "I was thinking that you probably want a break from this shallow gas, and I thought that a change of scenery might be good for you." Garth was only half listening as he continued transferring the data off of his computer; he was just waiting on the last one. "I was thinking maybe heavy oil would be a good change of pace for you."

Garth caught this last comment and he looked up at Pete. Heavy oil had a stigma about it. It was the place that Reservoir

Engineers went to die at Maldere. The reason for this was that heavy oil reserves were notoriously hard to forecast. The oil produced under cold production without steam relied on producing sand from the formation with the oil. The problem in forecasting was that once the sand stopped being produced, so did the oil, and it was anybody's guess when that would happen. Many a team had been burned at bonus time when a well or group of wells went to zero production with no advanced warning. Garth viewed this seemingly helpful suggestion from Pete as an insult.

"Thanks for the offer, Pete, but I think I will be moving along. You can take this as my two-week notice. I will be back later to get my stuff," said Garth. He ejected the disk and threw it in his briefcase with the others. Without giving Pete another glance, he stormed out of the office. For once in his life, Pete was speechless, and he just watched the back of Garth as he walked down the hall and pushed through the glass doors that led to the elevator bank.

After he reached the bottom floor, Garth walked through the revolving doors on street level. The day was warm. A beautiful fall day. Garth looked up to the sun and felt its warmth on his face. *Fall definitely was the best time of the year,* Garth thought. He wandered aimlessly through the downtown core, getting his thoughts in order. Everything was tumbling around him, and he felt totally useless. He walked up to the LRT platform to wait for the train to take him home. He knew no one would miss him at work, and he just didn't feel like being there. He sat at a bench to wait for the train. A voice over the public announcement speaker came on to say that due to a medical emergency, there was a fifteen-minute delay in all directions. *Great, just my luck,* thought Garth. His eyes were glossed over as he wallowed in his own pity, and he did not pay attention to the people who were milling about him on the platform. Many were voicing their displeasure about the train delay, but

Garth was in a daze. He kept his head down, rotating the owl pendant over and over in his hand.

Out of the corner of his eye, Garth could see a shock of white hair making its way through the crowd. He could see that the white hair was stopping to talk to every other person, and he knew that it was the same homeless guy that he usually saw in the morning. He did not have to look directly at him as Garth knew he would head straight for him. The man shuffled across the concrete platform and to Garth's surprise sat down right beside him on the bench.

The white-haired man let out a deep sigh of relief when he sat down. Garth was uneasy and nervous and tried his best to ignore the man. "Sure is hot today," said the man. Garth nodded and said "yep" but did not look in the direction of the man. "Hey 'big time', I see you quite often in the morning getting off on the first street platform, don't I?" said the man.

Garth turned his head to look at the man. *Of all the people he meets, he has to recognize me?* he thought. Garth for the first time actually considered the eyes of the man and studied his face. His sun-browned face showed numerous wrinkles under his eyes, small blue blood vessels were visible on his cheeks, and a white, long-haired beard surrounded his cracked lips. Garth looked into his blue-grey eyes and was surprised. Garth had always thought the man was old, but when he actually looked at him, he looked to be in his early fifties.

The man smiled and exposed his crooked and yellow teeth. The teeth had many gaps, but to Garth, it looked like he still had most of them. "I knew it," said the man. It was the man's turn to study Garth's face now, and he said, "You look like you just lost your best friend."

Garth turned his head back towards looking down the platform and in a far-off voice said, "I guess I have."

The man leaned back and extended his legs as if he was stretching and continued. "That is one of the gifts I have that suits me for my surroundings – years of looking into people's faces as they walk by me trying not to notice me has left me the ability to read people. I have a good feeling on who the people are to approach to ask for assistance and the ones to avoid all together. I know the kind of day people are having by how they move and carry themselves. One thing I have seen from all these years of observing people is that each time there are less and less people who seem to be happy."

Garth creased his forehead and looked back at the man.

"I could tell you were having one of those days as soon as I saw you," said the man. "You're an engineer, eh?" he asked as he gestured towards the iron ring on Garth's little finger on his right hand. "Does the price of natural gas have you down?" smiled the man. Garth shook his head. He acted like he was going to speak more, but then decided not to divulge any information. The man never took his eyes from Garth, and he spoke again., "You said you lost your best friend?"

Garth felt his eyes start to water again. *Jesus, not now, goddammitt,* he thought. Garth never usually liked talking to strangers, but this man had an air about him that calmed Garth, and before he could think better of it, he was spilling his guts.

He told the man all about working at Maldere, the death of the rig worker that was bothering him, the dilemma of working for lying and crooked people, as well as seeing his girlfriend with another man and how he had just quit his only job he had ever had outside of working on the farm. He told him how he felt like giving up and just heading back to Saskatchewan to get away from this place. When he was finished, the man leaned forward and placed his arms on his knees.

A train that was headed in Garth's direction pulled up to the station, and a crowd of people that had accumulated waiting for the trains to regain service pushed one another in front of the doors on the train. Garth watched as the people pushed and butted in front of one another to get aboard the train. Garth could see that the train was packed through the windows, and he had no ambitions of trying to squeeze himself into that sardine can.

"Sounds like you have experienced life, my friend," said the man. Garth just looked at him, snorted, and then looked away. Garth was watching as people were trying to move out of the way of the safety sensor eyes so that the door would close. One lady's dress kept getting in the way, and the door would partially close then open again. He heard the train driver's annoyed voice come over the intercom, "Please stand clear of the doors. We can't move until the doors close."

"Sorry, but what I mean by that is that life gives you all kinds of reasons to quit, but you have to find that thing that can keep you going," said the man.

Garth looked back at him incredulously and rudely said, "So says the hobo." The instant the words left Garth's lips, he regretted saying it.

The old man just smiled and said, "That's right. So says the hobo. If anyone should know, it is me."

Garth said, "I'm sorry, I didn't mean to offend you." The old man looked sympathetically at Garth and said, "No offense taken. It is true that I am homeless. But I wasn't always."

The old man looked down at his worn-out shoes on the bottom of his outstretched legs. "I don't really know anything about my mother. But I was told that she was a drug addict, and she had given me up for adoption. I bounced around from foster home to foster home ever since I can remember. I was abused at most of them, pretty much any way you can imagine. I learned at an early age how disgusting one human being can be to another. I would run away from these so-called homes and make my way on the streets. I would get busted from time to time for stealing, and I got messed up with heroin. Now and then I would end up in halfway houses, but I would always make it back to the streets."

The man paused, and Garth could see his eyes were getting misty. Then he sighed and continued, "Until one day I met the prettiest girl I had ever seen. She was at one of the halfway houses with me. She came from Lethbridge and had run away from her parents. We both struggled with drug addiction, but one day we decided that we deserved better from life. I convinced her to reconnect with her family. I moved with her to Lethbridge, and with some help from her parents, we were able to buy a piece of property with a mobile home. She found work as a waitress, and I worked for a pipeline construction company. We had some money, but the most valuable thing to me was being with her. She was everything to me." The man wiped away a tear.

Garth found that he was mesmerized as he listened intently to the old man's story. "What happened to her?" asked Garth.

The old man looked into Garth's face and continued. "We lived a great, happy life for ten years. We were even blessed with a son. Then one day it was over." Garth just looked at the man and pleaded with his eyes for him to continue. Finally, the man said, "They were killed by a drunk driver who blew through a stop sign on their way back from Edmonton. I was devastated, and before long, I found myself using again. I lost the trailer, lost my job, and was back here on the streets."

"They say that when you hit rock bottom, there is only one way to go. I would disagree. There are many ways you can go, but the hardest one is up again. I thought many times about ending my life. I came close one day on Centre Street bridge. But in that moment, before I was going to catapult myself off, I thought about my wife and son and decided that if I died, their memory would too. I knew she would not want that of me. I may be homeless still, but I am happy with what I do. I do my best to help out the other people I see on the street;

help them get the help they need to kick their drug habit or what have you. I learned to read people, to find the ones that truly need help. Most of the people you find here on the streets really deep down are good people and not the criminals that everyone thinks. Sometimes, the worst criminals in this town are the ones wearing a suit and tie who won't look these people in the eye." The old man finished and fidgeted with the belt that hung loosely under his belly.

"I am sorry about your wife and son," said Garth.

"Thank you, but I didn't tell you the story to look for your sympathy. Look, what I am saying is that it all comes down to choices. People say there are always two decisions that can be made for each ordeal we face – the right one and the wrong one. I say there are three – the right one, the wrong one, and no decision. The no decision is often worse than the wrong decision. Doing nothing will mess with your conscience worse than doing something and failing. So it goes with what happened with the rig worker. You feel worse by not trying something. Now I am not saying that it would have changed anything, but you would know that you tried. I am sure the next time you are faced with a similar situation, you will know what to do. Take solace in that and move on, or it will tear you up inside," said the old man.

Garth looked down at the dirty concrete platform and did not say anything as he was in deep thought. The old man then reached over and gently grasped his arm. Garth turned to look at the man. The man was smiling as he continued, "Also, you know about that guy that used you. He was a guy you mistrusted and didn't get along with from the start, right?"

Garth said, "Yes, what about him?"

The old man tilted his head and said, "You ever heard about the scorpion and the frog?" Garth shook his head. "The scorpion and the frog is a fable about a scorpion that asks a frog to carry it across a river. The frog of course says no, as it fears the scorpion will sting it. But the scorpion says that if it did that, they would both drown. The frog thinks about that and then decides it will take the scorpion across. Halfway across, the scorpion stings the frog, fating them both. The frog then asks why the scorpion stung him, and the scorpion replies, 'Because I am a scorpion, and that is what scorpions do.'" Garth drew his eyes away from the old man and back on the people on the platform. He was right. Heck, even Don Cherry used to say, "Never forget a friend, but never forget an enemy." That is exactly what Garth had done with Tyler. He should have known better.

Garth looked back at the man, and he gave him a weird look of understanding and shock. The old man saw this and laughed. "I don't mean to take this lightly, but all of the things that have you down are immaterial. Family and relationships are the most important." Garth nodded his head. "Believe me, this other shit in time will be a distant memory but losing someone who could be the love of your life is not easily forgotten and that, my friend, will weigh on you heavier than any of this other shit."

Garth's mind flashed to the phone conversation with his Dad. *Dad said the same*, he thought.

Another train pulled into the station. This train was a lot emptier than the previous one, but Garth decided to stay put. The train could wait. "But I don't have a job, and I can't let these guys get away with what they are doing," said Garth.

The old man sighed heavily and said, "Do you ever see old superheroes?"

Garth laughed, and confused, he said, "No."

"Have you ever thought about why?" asked the old man.

Again, Garth said, "Not really, but I would assume that it is because they have superpowers and have the ability to not grow old."

The old man leaned his head to the side and said, "Perhaps. But why I think you don't see old superheroes is because after all those years of fighting the wickedest villains of the world and receiving no credit for it, they start to wonder why they should fight anymore. Eventually they fade away or face becoming what they have lived a life fighting against. I mean, nobody appreciates that they have been fighting the good fight, and how do you determine who is good or bad? In real life, the wicked villain is not as obvious as in the comic books. Sometimes the people you think you are saving are no better than the ones you are trying to save them from. It's kind of like pissing your pants in the rain. It gives you a warm feeling momentarily, but your pants are still wet and nobody notices."

The old man noticed the frown on Garth's face and said, "Don't waste your life on strings better left to fray. Go get back your girl and worry about what you can control. You have the rest of your life to deal with assholes. Believe me the world will never run out of them."

Garth sat there shaking his head. "You're right. Thank you. Who knew that the smartest man I would meet in the big city is an old man on a bench waiting for a train."

The old man smiled a toothy grin and said, "You know, some of the dumbest people I have ever met are the ones with the most education because they never learned how to read people."

Another train pulled into the station, and the old man looked in its direction. "You better get on that one, rather than wasting the day talking to an old beggar." Garth looked at the train and saw that it was almost empty. Garth rose up and looked down at the man, "Thank you, sir. By the way, what is your name?"

The man smiled and said, "You can call me Joe. That is what my friends call me."

Garth extended his hand, and Joe clasped it and shook it. "Thank you, Joe. My name is Garth."

Joe said, "Nice to meet you, Garth. Now go get that lady, and don't be a stranger when I see you again."

"Certainly," said Garth as he turned and ran onto the train. He managed to climb aboard just as the doors started to close. He turned and waved to Joe sitting on the bench and ignored the look of the other patrons. He was sure they wondered why this person would be talking with some homeless beggar.

When the train finally arrived at the station where Garth had left his truck, he was starting to feel a little better about himself. He had been thinking a lot about what Joe had said to him. He also thought back to the conversations that he had with his dad and the indigenous man in Regina. He had tried calling Michelle numerous times, but she never picked up the phone or returned his messages. Now he was wondering how he was going to make things right with Michelle, and he hoped it wasn't too late. He knew that Michelle would still be at work, but he climbed in his truck and he headed over to her house.

As he drove through town to his destination, Garth passed a liquor store. He could really use a beer or three, he thought. He pulled his truck into the parking lot. The lot was empty, so he pulled up right in front of the door. As he shifted the truck into park, he suddenly realized he had left his wallet at the office, as he often took it out and put it into a drawer because it was uncomfortable to sit on all day. *I hope that bastard Stinky doesn't find that*, he thought. He rummaged through the centre console and found a bunch of loonies and toonies there. Thankfully, there looked like there would be enough to buy a poverty pack of some cheap beer.

He entered the store, and the bell chimed as the door was opened. The place was devoid of people except for the young lady standing at the till. She smiled and said "hello" as Garth walked in. He greeted her back and made his way to the beer cooler in the rear of the store. He opened the swinging door and felt the chill of the beer cooler as he looked around at the prices. He looked down at the gaggle of loonies and toonies in the palm of his hand. He did not have enough for his favourite Budweiser beer, but his eyes stumbled on a pack of Pilsner that he would be able to purchase with what little he had.

Garth scooped up the Pilsner beer and headed to the check-out. The girl at the counter smiled as he approached. Garth extended his hand to give her the change for the beer, and as she took the coins she said, "How long are you in town for?" Garth was startled by this comment, and he did not know what to say. She laughed at the confused look on his face and continued. "I assume you are from Saskatchewan as people from Saskatchewan are the only ones who buy Pilsner."

It was Garth's turn to laugh as he replied, "Ah. Well, I am from Saskatchewan originally, but I have been living in Calgary for a few years now."

The cashier exclaimed, "I knew it." Garth found himself smiling uncontrollably as she turned to place the change in the register. She said, "I am born and raised here, but my boy-friend is from Saskatoon and Pilsner is all he drinks." Garth smiled his acknowledgement and took up his pack of Pil and said thank you as he walked out of the store.

Knowing that Michelle would not be home, Garth decided he would write her a note and leave it in her door. He pulled up on the street beside her house and scribbled some words on an envelope he had found stuffed in the door of his truck. He walked up the steps, and as he was placing the envelope in the crack of the door, he heard barking coming from the other side of the door. "Omar, it's just me. Quiet," said Garth. Garth turned to leave, and the door opened and the envelope fell onto the ground.

A girl with long brown hair and a round face was stand-ing in the door. "What are you doing, Garth?" asked Sara,

Michelle's roommate. She was holding Omar in her arms, and he was still barking and struggling with all of his might to get to Garth. She set the dog down and stepped out onto the steps and closed the door leaving Omar inside where he continued to bark. She stooped down and picked up the envelope that had fallen on the ground. "What is this?" she said.

Sara, Garth knew was not his biggest fan. Garth guessed that it had something to do with her previous relationship with Tyler. He could tell from the unfriendly tone of her voice that this was not going to be a pleasant conversation. "I was just leaving something for Michelle," stammered Garth. Sara studied him up and down, and she looked down at the envelope in her hand. "Can you make sure she gets that," said Garth.

Sara glared back at Garth, and she rudely said, "You should give it to her yourself. I am not a delivery person."

Garth glared back at her and said, "Then put it back in the door if it is too much of a burden for you. I don't care what you think of me, but this is about me and her. And I would like her to read it herself."

Sara said, "It will be here, and she can read it if she wants to. But just so you know, she may not have time as she has a date tonight. I guess you were never that relevant as she is moving on." Garth glared at her. His lips were quivering, and he wanted to yell at her. Sara smiled and said, "I suggest you should move on too."

Garth was seething and he retorted, "Thank you for being so understanding, and thank you for your help. Just please make sure she gets it." He turned around, and without looking back to give Sara the satisfaction, climbed into his truck. As he sat down in the seat, he felt a sharp pain in his rear end. He reared up and looked down at what was the cause of the pain. It was the owl pendant that had somehow fallen down into his seat. He angrily gathered it up, and without thinking, hurled it at the door that Sara had disappeared behind. He threw the truck into gear and peeled out.

Garth's mind was racing but driving always seemed to be a way for him to collect his thoughts. Thinking of drinking, Garth looked down at the case of Pilsner sitting on the passenger side floor. He was just leaving the Calgary city limits, and he chuckled to himself as he thought of the times in high school when someone would say "far enough out of town" and then crack a beer.

He opened the glue seal of the top of the green, white, and red case and pulled out a long-necked brown bottle. He twisted off the cap and rolled down his window to throw the cap out. He admired the label. There was a lot going on in the scene on the label with a biplane, first nations and tepee, horse and buggy, old car, train, monks, and of course white rabbits. The Old Style Pilsner beer was often said to be from Saskatchewan, but Garth had always found it amusing to tell loyal drinkers of it that the beer actually originated from Lethbridge. The label actually played homage to much of the history of Lethbridge and Southern Alberta.

Garth looked over his shoulder to make sure the coast was clear and tilted the bottle skyward and took a good long drink. He felt the cold liquid running down his throat that burned ever so slightly. When he was finished, he held the bottle out and looked at the bubbles that had formed in the bottle over the clear brown liquid that remained. Most people would say that the beer was an acquired taste, but Garth momentarily savoured that malty sweet taste. Although it wasn't his favourite beer, on this day he was having he thought he had never tasted anything better.

Garth continued to drive down Highway 1, east from Calgary. He had gotten the radio fixed, and he was listening to the *Exit O* cassette from Steve Earle and the Dukes. Garth played one song over and over as he drove and drank suds. The song was "I Ain't Ever Satisfied". The song had been released quite a few years ago but did not chart very high. Garth was surprised by this, as he thought it was one of the greatest songs he had ever heard. Other songs if you played them too much would lose their appeal to you, but this song was one that Garth could listen to over and over and never tire of.

After a couple of hours, Garth finally neared his destination. He pulled off the highway and drove down the gravel road that lead to the Copper Canyon field. When he reached the top of the hill that looked down over the field, he pulled the truck off to the side of the road. He surveyed the scene below him. Where once he had seen a beehive of activity, he could see only one drilling rig standing and only a handful of vehicles milling about. He looked out over the prairie and could see the scars left over from the pipelines that had been laid down. In the distance, he could see the compressor station, and even from this range, he could see there was only one compressor running as there was only the one cooler fan spinning. The others sat idle with tumbleweeds piled up in the screens.

The sun was going down, and the prairie was lit up in a warm golden glow. He could see the cliffs along the river where many years ago the Blackfoot tribes had run some of the thousands of buffalo that used to roam here over the cliffs where waiting tribe members would finish off the animals that weren't immediately killed by the fall. He thought about how this area must have looked before the settlers came to this area. Even with the beauty before him, he thought of how one of the first foreign travellers to this area, John Palliser, had declared this area unsuitable for agriculture and essentially a wasteland. No one had known at that time what lay below the surface.

Garth sat there looking around in all directions. There were gas wells dotted all over the hill sides, and their black skeletons of insulated pipe could be seen scattered all through the grass. Rudyard Kipling, the English author of the *Jungle Book*, had declared this land had "all hell for a basement" because of the immense reserves of natural gas. Garth chuckled to himself as he thought, *Hell may not freeze over, but the basement is flooded in places.*

Garth continued driving down the road. He came to an approach that had a sign hanging on the fence. It had the well locations that could be accessed down this trail. Garth's eyes set on the one that said 9-33. This was the well that Darren Heywood had been killed at. He parked the truck and walked on to the well site. In the centre of the lease was a piece of pipe sticking out of the ground with a valve and a bull plug in the end of it. The grass around the well head was still laid flat to the ground as evidence where the rig and equipment had sat while the well was drilled. There was no marker or sign that showed the evidence of the tragic event that had transpired here; only this rusting pipe and valve sticking out of the ground, to which a young man had given his life.

Garth finished off the bottle of beer he was carrying and hurled it at that ugly piece of iron. The bottle struck the valve and shattered, flaying glass in all directions. The pipe stood defiantly as the liquid evaporated off its steel exterior.

Garth climbed back into his truck and returned out onto the highway. He drove a few more kilometres and then pulled over at the turnout on the side of the road beneath the sign that read "First Discovery of Natural Gas". He read and re-read the words on display there as he drank his beer. As Garth sat there, he suddenly realized he was physically and mentally exhausted. He tilted his seat back to a more comfortable position, and using an old coat for a pillow, leaned his head against the window and slept.

Nightfall had fallen when Garth was startled awake by frantic banging on his driver's side window. Being awoken from a deep sleep, Garth looked about from side to side as he tried to understand the situation. Eyes still sleepy, he saw that it was completely dark around him, save for the headlights that shone in his rear-view mirror. Blindly he fumbled around for the button to roll down the window. Before he could reach the switch, his door flew open, and there standing before him was the most beautiful redhead he had ever laid eyes on.

"Thank God I found you," exclaimed Michelle, and she reached into the truck and embraced Garth in a deep hug.

Garth was blinking his eyes and trying to shake out the cobwebs. Was he dreaming this? "You had me worried to death with that letter you left. Your dad called me and was frantic about where you were. And when I found this, I thought you were going to harm yourself," she exclaimed. She was holding his owl pendant in her hand. Even in the darkness, he could see that there was a piece missing from the bottom of it where it had struck the door.

"I thought you had a date tonight," Garth said mockingly. Everything was starting to flood back to him now as he was regaining his senses.

"Of course not. Who told you that?" she said.

"Sara," said Garth.

"Forget about anything that she says. She is just bitter about her life and takes it out on everyone else," she said. "I told you I love you, you dumb bastard."

This time, Garth looked into her eyes and he could see they were blood-shot and her eyelashes were soaked from crying. "I quit my job. That asshole Tyler used me so that him and Kane could takeover Maldere," he stammered.

"We have plenty of time to talk about that. Let's get you out of here though before you get arrested for an impaired," she said as she looked down at the empty bottles on the floor. "Leave your truck here and climb in with me," she said.

"Didn't you hear me? My career is over," exclaimed Garth. She looked at him sympathetically, and she said, "Your career has just begun. There are other companies that are way better than Maldere, and we will figure out what to do with Tyler. But right now, you only have to worry about me, as I am going to kick your ass if you don't get in the car right now."

A smile trickled across his lips. She always had a way with words. "I love you more than anything. I really don't know what I would do without you," said Garth. Michelle grabbed the sides of Garth's head and pulled him into her, and their lips locked in a long emotional kiss. She took up his hand in hers and led him back to her running car. "Come on, Jimmy. There is a hotel somewhere with our name on it."

THE END

J.D. Knibbs grew up in small town Saskatchewan. In his twenties, he moved to Calgary, where he has worked in petroleum engineering for over twenty years. *Unconventional Beginnings* loosely resembles his own experiences in the oil patch and is his first novel.

Mr. Knibbs lives with his wife and two boys in Okotoks, a town in the Province of Alberta, Canada, approximately eighteen kilometers south of the City of Calgary.

CPSIA information can be obtained
at www.ICGtesting.com
Printed in the USA
LVHW021948160320
650236LV00001B/8